THE

LOST

PENDANT

by Suzie Jay

The Gulrose Kingdom lies in the northern region of Mörkdimma, where Amara was born seventeen years ago.

Her childhood was not as pleasant as one might expect for a princess, with her father not loving her right and her mother dying during childbirth - or so Amara thought.

This book is for anyone who has ever dreamed of escaping to a land of magic - riding unicorns through the skies, battling in enchanted forests, and falling in love with someone who would set the world ablaze for the

Glombort
Gulrose
Morkdimma
Gulrose Forest
Dodblomma Forest
Melak Forest
Arid Ravine
Skadlig
Dodblomma

Chapter 1 : Mystery Girl...1

Chapter 2 : The Secret Kingdom 17

Chapter 3 : Finding Annabel 35

Chapter 4 : Finding Catherine 45

Chapter 5 : The Art Of Witchcraft................61

Chapter 6 : Betrayal 75

Chapter 7 : Reunion 89

Chapter 8 : A Horrible Secret...................105

Chapter 9 : The Girl In The Woods 125

Chapter 10 : Diaries From The Dead...........147

Chapter 11 : Spilled Blood 161

Chapter 12 : The Hunter............................ 181

Chapter 13 : The Forbidden Love...............201

Chapter 14 : Imprisonment.......................215

Chapter 15 : The Secret Child 229

Chapter 16 : The Unexpected Arrival..........241

Chapter 17 : The Crossover 255

Chapter 18 : The Day Before 277

Chapter 19 : The Day Of 295

Chapter 20 : The Day After 309

Chapter 21 : Sacrifice 327

Chapter 22 : Unravelling Of The Secrets 341

Chapter 23 : The Truth Always Comes Out ..361

Chapter 24 : The Forest Of The Dead 379

Chapter 25 : The Ravine 393

Chapter 26 : The Supreme One 409

CHAPTER 1

Mystery Girl

For a week, Henry Newmann found himself captivated by a beautiful girl on the train he took home from his favourite place in the world—the Warrington Library, where he worked. There was something about her that held his attention, something beyond her striking appearance. An inexplicable sense of connection stirred within him, and he couldn't help but be drawn to her, fascinated by the mystery she seemed to carry.

She would simply stand there, even when seats were available, staring blankly ahead until she got off the train.

She had long, silky, dark brown hair and forest-green eyes. She wore black skinny jeans, a white shirt, and a dark blue jacket. A grey hat rested on her head, paired with black boots and small silver earrings shaped like hearts. On her index finger, she wore a very strange ring—it was large and green, with a cross in the middle. Henry had never seen a ring like that before; it looked very old, as if it belonged in one of the old movies he used to watch with his mum.

Henry was a tall, skinny eighteen-year-old boy with short brown hair and dark brown eyes that sometimes seemed almost black under bright light. He was dressed in his usual black jeans, a black Nirvana shirt, a brown jacket, and brown trainers.

He was trying to gather the courage to speak to the girl. He didn't know anything about her, but he liked to imagine what her life might look like. He didn't know that her name was Amara, and he definitely didn't know that she didn't belong there. She didn't belong in his world; she was only there to find her mother and bring her back home—to their world.

But let's start from the beginning.

Amara was born in a distant land called Mörkdimma, home to the most beautiful kingdom anyone had ever seen: the Gulrose Kingdom. She was born into a royal family, and her father was the King, which, of course, made her a princess.

Mörkdimma was not a place you would ever hear of; it wasn't anywhere in or near the human world.

You couldn't simply take a train or a plane to get there—only magic could take you.

Amara travelled to London with the help of her teacher, a great sorcerer named Theodore, who gave her a task she needed to fulfil to save herself, her mother, and the entire kingdom from a terrible future. She had to find her mother, who had left their land only hours after Amara was born, seventeen years ago.

Theodore told Amara a story she had never heard before—the true story of what had happened to her mother. He revealed everything she needed to know about her birth and how she came to be a princess.

Her mother, Catherine, had fallen in love with King William, Amara's father. He was a tall, stocky man with dark hair and light brown eyes—very handsome, though his heart was dark. He wasn't the most beloved king, caring little for his people and far too much for gold and power, but Catherine didn't see that. She believed he was kind and caring, and he could be—sometimes, but only to her.

Catherine's beauty was an obsession for William, one that made him a better man whenever they were together. She held a power over him that no one could explain, and William would do anything to make her happy and content.

However, the same could not be said of his people, who had suffered tremendously under his hunger for power since his coronation.

When William's father passed away, William and his twin brother, Peter, were forced to duel for the crown at just twenty-three years old. The day before the duel, Peter came to speak to William. Peter, a kind brother beloved by all, wanted only the best for his people. He told William that, no matter who won the fight, they could rule side by side and transform the Gulrose Kingdom into a place where the people would prosper and live happily.

But William felt differently. He cared little for the happiness of others. His main concern was the kingdom's vault, which held little gold. William wanted to be the richest man alive, respected and feared by all. He dreamed of his enemies trembling at the mere mention of his name.

Before the duel began, the two brothers swore an oath to obey the royal rules of combat: no one would be gravely injured, and they would fight fairly. It was a close match, as both brothers were excellent swordsmen; however, in the end, Peter emerged victorious.

His triumph meant he was to become the next king of the Gulrose Kingdom. The people celebrated, as they all wanted him to succeed. They believed he would care for them and their families, and that he would stand by them, protecting them from all harm.

Their excitement did not last long. On the morning of his coronation, Peter was found dead in his bed. The people soon learned he had been poisoned, though the murderer was never found. Some speculated it was William's doing, believing he had killed his own brother to seize the crown. Everyone knew of his desire to rule.

It was at William's coronation ball that he first met Catherine.

She had travelled to the Gulrose Kingdom to meet the new king and celebrate his accession, accompanied by her father, the King of Dodblomma, who had been a close friend of William's father for many years. From the moment he saw her, he knew he wanted her. She was strikingly beautiful, and William believed that every king needed a beautiful queen by his side.

Her kingdom's wealth also tempted him; Dodblomma's treasury was abundant with gold, and by marrying her, William's financial troubles would vanish.

Her father also commanded a large army, which would be a valuable addition to William's own forces and would solve yet another problem he faced.

The two of them danced, talked, and got to know each other all night. By the end of the evening, William asked Catherine to stay in his castle a while longer so they could deepen their connection. After a week, he asked her father for his blessing to marry

Catherine, and her father agreed. Catherine was ecstatic; she believed her future would be a perfect fairy tale. But she couldn't have been more wrong.

Within four weeks, they were married, and everyone expected Catherine to become pregnant quickly. But as weeks turned into months, no heir was born to the kingdom. Catherine grew desperate. The King often reminded her that, as Queen, it was her duty to provide him with an heir. She feared that if she didn't, he would find someone who would. Catherine was prepared to do anything to have a child, no matter the cost.

She searched for someone who could grant her what she wanted most, and eventually, she found such a person—one she would soon regret ever seeking out. She found the last known witch in the Gulrose Kingdom, a woman named Agnes.

Once, witches had been common and well-respected in the kingdom. But by the time Catherine sought out Agnes, most had disappeared or been killed during the rule of William's father, Leopold.

Leopold had become convinced that the witches would destroy the kingdom and harm his family, so he set out to eliminate as many of them as he could. You might wonder how he managed to do it.

Leopold came from an ancient royal family with a dark history—they were all shapeshifters. Each could transform into a manticore: a lion with bat-like wings and a scorpion's tail. Manticores were strong, incredibly fast, and not easily angered; but once provoked, they were ruthless.

There were only two ways to become a manticore. You were either born one, or you had to be stung by one—a process that was agonising.

A sting from a manticore's tail would bring hours of unbearable pain, fever, and severe hallucinations. Victims would do anything to escape the torment, even if it meant harming those closest to them. That's how intolerable the suffering was.

Years ago, Leopold and his army had slaughtered nearly all the witches in the kingdom. The only one who survived or didn't flee was Agnes, hidden by her mother's powerful spell before she herself was killed.

Everyone knew the story, including Catherine. She had no idea if Agnes would be willing to help her after all the shapeshifters had done to the witches. Agnes might even want to harm Catherine. But desperate to conceive a child of royal blood, Catherine was willing to risk her life to try.

One stormy night, Catherine ventured deep into the Gulrose woods to find Agnes's home. After hours of travel through the heavy rain, she found it, hidden deep within the Dark Forest. When she knocked on the door, Agnes already knew why the Queen had come.

She invited Catherine in and, to Catherine's surprise, promised to help her.

In exchange, Agnes asked only for an open payment, meaning she could call on Catherine for a favour at any time. Driven by her desperation, the Queen agreed.

Agnes prepared a potion, assuring Catherine it would fulfil her dream of becoming a mother. As

Catherine held the potion in her hand, she hesitated. But her longing for a child outweighed her doubt, and she placed it in her coat before leaving.

The next night, she drank the potion before going to bed with the King. When she awoke in the morning, her heart raced with excitement. She knew it would take time to confirm a pregnancy, but she was certain the potion would work—it simply had to. After a month, the kingdom finally received the joyful news: the Queen was pregnant. Celebrations erupted, but no one was more pleased than the King. At last, he would have an heir—and another manticore to fight in his name.

Yet even with her wish granted, the Queen couldn't shake an unease that lingered like a shadow. She now owed a favour to Agnes, a witch who despised anyone outside her own kind. She had no idea what the payment might be, but she prayed it would be simple, allowing her to raise her child in peace.

In her heart, she knew she would love her son or daughter more than anything and could hardly wait to become a mother.

One night, when the Queen was asleep, she heard a strange noise coming from the nursery that had been prepared for her unborn child.

She got up and walked to the nursery. When she opened the door, she saw a person standing there, playing with little white unicorns that were hanging above the crib. It was Agnes. The Queen was startled; she didn't understand why the witch was there unannounced, but she guessed she had come to claim her payment. Composing herself, Catherine stood tall, determined not to show fear.

"I've come to let you know what I will take for helping you make your dream come true," said Agnes, her voice low and ominous.

"What is it?" asked the Queen, her confidence faltering under the witch's dark gaze.

Agnes fixed her eyes on Catherine. "The child you carry, of course. She will be born with a gift—a powerful one. And on her eighteenth birthday, I will come to take her away with me. Together, we will rebuild the coven your kingdom tried to destroy, the one your King sought to erase."

The Queen was paralysed with fear. She struggled to grasp Agnes's words. What gift? What did she mean, take her child away? And how did she know it would be a daughter, not a son? A chill ran down her spine, and in that moment, all her bravery dissolved, replaced by a terror she had never felt before.

"I added something extra special to that little potion I gave you," Agnes said, her voice laced with cold satisfaction.

"A spell that will grant your daughter powers—like mine, but far greater. And if you want her to survive such strength, you will let me take her. Remember, my Queen: when she turns eighteen, I will come for her. Consider this time with her my gift to you, and rest assured—I will take very good care of her." With those words, Agnes vanished.

The Queen sank to her knees, tears pouring down her face. How could she have fallen for the witch's game?

She returned to her bed, silently vowing to do everything in her power to protect her daughter from

Agnes. Whatever it took, she would not allow the witch to take her child.

Catherine searched tirelessly for a way to defeat the witch. When every book failed to yield answers and she had nowhere else to turn, she confided in Theodore, the only person she trusted. A few days later, he returned with a glimmer of hope.

"There may be a way," he told her. "A very old pendant, one capable of capturing magical power. If we can find it, we could trap the witch's powers within it. She would be powerless to take your daughter—or to harm anyone else ever again."

There was a catch, however: the pendant was lost in a land without magic or witches. Its people considered manticores mere myths, and magic nothing more than a fantasy.

Theodore explained to Catherine that the pendant had been crafted by a powerful witch named Merla, who died at the hands of William's father. In her final act, Merla sent the pendant away with her only daughter, hoping to protect them both from harm.

But Theodore's powers were limited; he could only send

Catherine to this land without magic on her own, without the means to bring her back. Her only hope of returning to defeat Agnes lay with her unborn daughter. If Agnes's prediction proved true, Catherine's daughter would one day possess the power to retrieve her and imprison Agnes's magic within the pendant.

The Queen was devastated. She didn't want to leave her daughter to be raised solely by the King, but she had no choice. To save her child, she had to go.

Seventeen years later, Amara would discover the truth about her mother's fate.

Until then, Catherine and Theodore concealed the truth, making it appear that the Queen had died giving birth to Amara. In reality, Theodore had sent her to London—the last known location of the pendant.

When Amara learned the truth, she could barely comprehend it. All her life, she'd believed her mother was dead, only to discover she was alive—

waiting in another world for her daughter to bring her home.

She knew she had to search for her mother, but the questions haunted her: Did Catherine even survive? Had she found what she was looking for?

Theodore shared everything he knew about this foreign land. He told her she didn't have to be afraid. He would cast a spell on her, and no one would be able to see her. Only those who truly believed in magic would be able to see her, and this place was filled with non-believers.

CHAPTER 2

The Secret Kingdom

Henry gathered all his courage to speak to Amara.

When they both stepped off the train at Whitechapel Station, he approached her.

"Hey, do you need help?"

He didn't expect her reaction. She turned around, looking scared—petrified even. Then she said the strangest thing to him.

"Y... you can see me?" Amara asked.

"Of course, I can see you."

Amara glanced around, as if trying to determine whether anyone else could see her. She was bewildered. Did this mean he believed in magic?

After a brief silence, he asked again, "Can I help you? I'm Henry. Nice to meet you."

Amara looked like she was trying to collect herself

before replying coldly, "I am Amara and no, thank you. I don't need your help," she said as she started walking away, cautiously glancing around.

Henry noticed she was different from the other people around him. She was dressed normally, but her demeanour set her apart from him and his friends. He couldn't explain it, but she seemed like she didn't belong in this place.

Despite her rejection, he knew he couldn't just leave her there. He decided to keep his distance while still sticking around for a bit to make sure she was okay. He followed closely behind her and noticed she kept turning around to see if he was still there.

He wondered if she had run away or if she was in some kind of trouble and maybe was trying to hide out.

Finally, he approached her again.

"Please, let me help you. I live here and know this area well. Where are you trying to get to?"

"This is Wh... Whitechapel, right?" Amara asked.

"Yes, it is. Where exactly do you need to go?"

"I need to find someone, but I don't know where exactly that person lives. I just got instructions that this was one of the places she could be," she replied.

"Okay, so you're looking for a random person and you don't know where they live. Should be easy enough," he said sarcastically. Then he added, "I'll try to help you, but first, we should get somewhere warm. C'mon, I know a great place nearby."

Amara glanced around and, out of desperation, she agreed. She had been searching for her mother for days and had no leads. Maybe he could help her— he was from this world and knew much more than she did.

They entered a small coffee shop on the corner of Whitechapel Road and sat down. Henry ordered two hot chocolates. An awkward silence settled between them at first. Amara kept glancing at the front door as if expecting someone to walk in, looking a little paranoid. Henry decided not to press her for answers about her behaviour.

"Here are your hot chocolates. I hope your friend will arrive soon, so they don't get cold," said the waitress as she brought over their drinks. Henry was confused. Amara was sitting right there.

"Okay, you have to tell me everything I need to know so I can help you," he insisted.

"I can't tell you everything. I have secrets that are mine alone to keep—for everyone's safety," Amara replied.

Henry decided he would accept this for now. He thought that maybe if he shared some things about himself, it might make her trust him a bit more, and she would feel more comfortable sharing some of her life with him.

He told her he lived with his mother, Mary, a petite woman with dirty blonde hair that fell to her shoulders and brown eyes. His father had passed away when he was just a baby. According to his mother, it was a horrible car accident. She didn't talk about it much because it was too painful.

Whenever he asked her to tell him more about it, his mother would brush him off. He told Amara that he always felt like he didn't belong. He had friends, but he was different. He believed in things others didn't, and that made him feel like an outsider.

They sat and talked for hours. Well, Henry did most of the talking. He spoke about places he wanted to go and the library where he worked.

All of this seemed to work; Amara began to talk to him a bit more openly. There was a feeling inside her that she could trust him, so she decided to share more about why she was there. Maybe, just maybe, he might be able to help her find her mother. First, she told him she was surprised to find a believer here because she had been told there were none.

Henry looked puzzled and asked, "What do you mean by a believer?"

"Well, that's the thing. You're not supposed to see me unless you believe in magic."

At first, Henry wanted to laugh, but seeing how serious she was, he stopped himself.

"Okay then," said Henry. After taking a deep breath, he continued, "So, no one else here can see you?"

"Well, I don't know," said Amara. "Unless they believe in magic, they won't. But let's try, shall we?"

She stood up and walked over to an elderly man sitting at the counter, eating a scone and sipping a cup of tea. She started talking to him, waving her hand in front of his face, but the old man had no reaction. It was as if Amara weren't there. She repeated this with a few more people to prove she wasn't lying. After a while, Henry finally believed her—well, at least a little bit.

Amara sat back down and began telling him about her father and mother. She explained how her mother had fallen pregnant with her, about the evil witch, and how her mother had faked her own death and sacrificed everything to save her. She described how her mother had travelled to London to search for Merla's lost pendant.

After what seemed like an eternity, Henry sat there in complete disbelief. His eyes were wide open, and he didn't say a word.

His mind was spinning. If all of this was true, his desire to help her grew even stronger. He knew it wouldn't be easy, but he felt prepared to do whatever it took to assist her. He didn't know why, but if anyone were to ask him to describe his soulmate, he would describe her. It was a strange feeling he had never experienced before—a deep, inexplicable sense that he would do anything for her without question.

They left the now-empty coffee shop and walked around for a while. Amara shared more about her homeland, and Henry listened eagerly. He had always been fascinated by knights, kingdoms, witches, and everything magical, and now it seemed all of it was real. His world had just opened up to so many new possibilities.

It was October in London, so the air was cold and windy. They were enjoying their walk when Amara abruptly stopped.

"What is it?" Henry asked.

"Someone is following us," she replied. "I noticed him when we were in the coffee shop. He was staring at us, and now I see him again."

Henry turned to see who she was talking about, and sure enough, a young man around his age was standing there, watching them.

"Just ignore him. I'm sure it's just a coincidence," Henry said.

Amara's hands were shaking, her eyes wide with fear. "No, please trust me. We have to run—now."

They picked up their pace, and so did he. Within moments, they were running, and every time they turned a corner, he increased his speed to match theirs.

They hid behind a building, thinking they had lost him, when he suddenly appeared behind them. He shoved Henry to the ground as if it were nothing, and Henry's head smashed against the cold, hard pavement. The man grabbed Amara and dragged her away. Terrified, she tried to fight back, then she screamed—so loudly that Henry had to cover his ears. Her eyes filled with a bright blue light.

Suddenly, it was as though something—or someone—pulled the man away. He flew metres from Amara and slammed into a nearby wall, hitting his head and passing out. Henry quickly got to his feet, grabbed Amara's hand, and they ran to his flat.

He only lived a few minutes away. By the time they reached the front of his building, they were both out of breath and visibly shaken.

"What was that? How did you do that?" Henry asked, his voice trembling.

"I have magic, Henry, but I don't always know how to control it properly," Amara replied, her voice trembling.

Henry squeezed her hand and led her inside his flat. "C'mon, we'll be safe here. You can tell me more inside."

When they walked in, Henry's mother was making dinner. With her back to them, she turned to greet her son, but as she did, the bowl of salad she had been holding slipped from her hands and shattered on the floor.

She had a look of horror on her face, as though she had seen a ghost. Amara and Henry were shocked by her reaction. Another person could see her—Henry's mother believed in magic.

Mary began to clean up the glass, muttering to herself as she worked. After a moment, she stood up and said, "What are you doing here?"

Amara furrowed her brows. "I'm sorry. You know who I am?"

"Yes, I know who you are. You look exactly like your mother."

"You know my mother? Do you know where she is?" Amara asked urgently.

"We have a lot to talk about. Come and sit," Mary said, gesturing for them to follow her to the kitchen table.

As they sat down, Mary began to share her side of the story. She revealed that Henry's father hadn't died in a car accident but had been murdered. She didn't disclose who had killed him or why she was so afraid. She explained that Theodore was the one who had sent them to London and had continued to send her messages, updating her on everything that had been happening. Mary had hoped that one day it would be safe to reveal the truth to Henry and return home—to the Kingdom of Gulrose.

She told Amara that while she might have known how she came to be born and about her mother's deal with the witch, she didn't know what had happened before her mother left the land. Yes, it was true that nearly all the witches in Gulrose had been wiped out; however, a few had managed to hide. A handful of witches were scattered across the kingdom, and when Agnes made her deal with the Queen, word spread. Gulrose began to seem safe for witches once more. They returned and gradually took control of many villages.

The King hid Amara in the castle, keeping her unaware of what was happening. He began to lose his mind at the thought of his only heir being a witch. He despised witches deeply and was determined to eradicate every last one of them.

"Theodore cast a spell that sent us here. I knew we wouldn't be able to return to our land—perhaps never—but I had to keep my son safe," Mary explained.

Henry was shocked and a little angry. Why had his mother never told him any of this? He was eighteen and had lived his whole life without ever hearing this story. He had lived his whole not knowing where he was really born.

Amara told Mary about the man who had been chasing them earlier and admitted she had accidentally used her powers to help them escape.

Mary asked them to describe the man, and when they did, she immediately recognised him and understood his purpose. She told them that Theodore's most recent message to her had been about Amara and her quest. He had warned her that Agnes had sent a hunter to capture Amara and bring her back.

The hunter wouldn't harm Amara, but he would kill anyone who stood in his way. If he found them there, he would kill Mary and Henry before taking Amara back to their land for Agnes.

Amara was confused. Theodore had made it seem as though travelling between the two lands was nearly impossible, yet it appeared he had helped others reach this world. Did that mean Theodore had been lying? Why hadn't he warned her about the hunter? He could have sent her a message the same way he had done with Mary. Could she trust everything he had told her?

Overwhelmed, Amara began to tremble. This was all too much. She had felt this way before, and it never ended well. She knew that if she lost control, she could hurt Henry or Mary—and that was the last thing she wanted.

Suddenly, she bolted out the front door.

"Amara? Amara! Come back!" Henry shouted as he leapt to his feet and ran after her.

It was already dark, and she didn't know the area; she didn't even know this land. He cared for her, and he didn't want anything bad to happen to her. He looked around the street, and just when he started to lose hope of finding her, he heard it—very faint sobs. They were coming from behind an abandoned building. Henry followed the sound and found Amara.

She was sitting on the ground, staring at her hands, shaking—not from the cold, but from fear. Henry approached her and knelt down in front of her. Before he could say anything, Amara spoke first.

"I didn't mean to—I didn't mean to do it. He just wanted to help me, but I couldn't control it. I was upset."

Henry was confused and didn't understand what she was talking about. He looked in the direction she was facing, and his eyes widened in terror. There was a man lying on the ground, covered in blood; his eyes were open, and blood was pouring from them.

"Amara, what happened? Did you do this?" Henry asked cautiously.

"I didn't mean to. I don't know what happened. I'm sorry; I'm so, so sorry," she cried.

She had killed him. Of course, she hadn't done it on purpose, but that didn't change the fact that the man was now dead. Henry took Amara's hand and led her away. He wanted to bring her back to his flat, but

Amara didn't want to go; she couldn't face his mother after what she had just done.

Henry had one other person he could trust with anything: his old history teacher, Arthur Collins. Arthur had joined Henry's secondary school when Henry was thirteen, and they had immediately hit it off. They talked about history and fiction. Arthur was particularly interested in witchcraft, werewolves, vampires, and other folklore.

They enjoyed each other's company, and when Henry left school, they stayed in contact and met a few times a week. Henry knew Arthur was very open-minded, and if anyone could help them, it would be him.

After a short walk, Amara and Henry arrived at Arthur's house. He lived nearby, and Henry was always welcome there. They knocked on the door, and a short, chubby, grey-haired man opened it, looking surprised to see Henry at this late hour.

"Hi, Henry, what are you doing here? And who is this—your friend?" asked Arthur, puzzled at the sight of Henry and his companion.

"Good evening, Arthur. I was wondering if we could come in and talk to you," Henry asked politely.

"Of course, my boy, come on in."

Henry walked in with Amara, who followed closely behind. Both were surprised that Arthur could see her, but they were also glad; this would make the story more believable. They sat down at the dining table, and Arthur started making them tea. It was awkwardly quiet in Arthur's dining room. They began drinking their tea, and Henry told Arthur the story of their night. He didn't leave anything out, except for the unfortunate incident Amara had with that man—who was now dead. By the end, after everything had come out, he felt silly. Not because it wasn't true, but because it sounded so made up. The great thing about Arthur was that he was, in fact, a believer. He believed in the impossible. He listened to Henry with full attention, and once Henry had finished telling his story, Arthur said,

"I believe you, Henry."

"You do?"

"Yes, I do, and I believe I can help you find this pendant you were talking about," said Arthu

CHAPTER 3

Finding Annabel

Henry looked at Arthur with a confused but intrigued expression. How could Arthur possibly help him?

Arthur explained that the story of Merla's lost pendant was quite famous in their world. It was said to be the most beautiful piece of jewellery on Earth. Of course, no one had ever seen it; it was simply another piece of folklore that Arthur loved to read about.

According to the legend, it belonged to a very powerful witch named Merla. She fell in love with a human, and they were supposed to get married; they couldn't have been happier to start their lives together.

Unfortunately, on the night of their wedding, Merla's mother killed her lover just minutes before the ceremony, as she didn't want her daughter to marry a human. Using her magic, she ripped out his heart and buried it in the deepest part of the woods so her daughter would never find it and could never bring him back. Merla was heartbroken, filled with grief and anger. Using her powers, she created a pendant adorned with golden embellishments, tiny golden roses, and a green centrepiece. It was so beautiful; it was almost enchanting. She trapped her mother's powers within it so she could never hurt anyone again, then she locked her mother away, never to be seen again.

Merla always wore the pendant as a reminder of her first and only love, but one day, both she and the necklace disappeared. No one ever discovered what happened to her, but it was speculated that she had run away to this world to find happiness, as she had been spotted here in the late 1800s. Arthur always thought of this as just another fairy tale; however, now he believed it might actually be true. An explorer at heart, he didn't hesitate to offer Henry his services. He began packing a backpack as they talked more about where Amara's mother might be.

Did she find the pendant? And if so, had she been waiting for Amara this whole time, all on her own?

Arthur gave Henry a book containing the story of Merla. The book was titled *The True Story of Folklore from Far Away* and was authored by an unknown writer.

It included everything Arthur had already shared with Henry and Amara, but it also mentioned that after escaping Gulrose, Merla had apparently lived in Whitechapel from 1895. Not much was known about her life among humans; however, she did find love. She married a human in 1900 when she was twenty-five, and they had a daughter named Ella when she was twenty-nine. Later, Ella had a daughter named Annabel in 1924.

While reading this story, Henry had an idea. If they could track down Merla's grandchild, Annabel, they might be able to find the pendant—or at least discover whether Catherine had come to her. Jewellery with such a rich history often gets passed down within families. With that in mind, they began their search. They estimated that Annabel would be around seventy-six years old and might still have the pendant.

They went to her last known address, where a short, freckled, middle-aged woman answered the door.

"Yes? Can I help you?" she asked.

"Hi, my name is Henry, and this is my friend Arthur. We were wondering if we could speak with Annabel Riley?" he asked, a note of hope in his voice.

The woman explained that Annabel was the previous owner of the house and had sadly passed away a few years ago. She mentioned that she had purchased the property at an auction. Seeing the disappointment on their faces, she listened as they told her they were distant relatives of Annabel and had hoped to reconnect with her.

When they asked if any of Annabel's possessions had been left behind, the woman told them about a box of her belongings stored in the attic. While she didn't trust them enough to let them into her house, she offered to bring the box out for them, mentioning that she would have donated it to charity otherwise. Though not what they had hoped for, they were somewhat pleased to have found something. As they sifted through the box, they found no trace of the pendant. Instead, they came across Annabel's diaries. Intrigued, they began reading entries from around the time Amara's mother had arrived— seventeen years ago. If Catherine had been searching for the pendant, perhaps she had visited Annabel.

Their hunch proved correct. Among the pages, they discovered detailed accounts of Catherine's first visit. Catherine had approached Annabel to share the story of Agnes and Amara. Annabel, knowing her family's history and the pendant's powers, had listened intently.

Annabel did have her mother's jewellery, but she couldn't bear to part with it. It held immense sentimental value and was incredibly powerful.

However, Catherine's story was so heartbreaking that Annabel found herself unable to refuse. She wanted to help Amara.

"So, my mother found the pendant?" Amara asked.

"It looks like it," Henry replied.

"Well, if she found it, then the only thing left to do is find her and go home," Amara said.

Henry's expression grew sombre. Of course, he wanted Amara to find her mother, but once she did, it would likely mean he'd never see her again. Then, a spark of hope flickered in his mind.

Maybe he could go with her. After all, he and his mother were from that world, so perhaps it was possible. Would his mother even agree? She had mentioned wanting to return home one day.

His thoughts were cut short by Arthur, who reminded them that they didn't have much time left. Henry explained that Amara only had a week to find her mother, bring her back home, and confront Agnes.

What do you do in this situation? What is the best plan you can come up with when you're looking for someone and have no idea where to start?

They packed all the diaries into Arthur's backpack and began walking back to his place. Once there, they sat down and continued reading. Perhaps Ann had written something about where Catherine was staying, or maybe she had mentioned where she was planning to go next.

After hours of poring over the diaries, just when they were about to give up, Amara found something. While it didn't specify where her mother was staying, it mentioned a man who had been helping her with her quest. His name was Nicholas Moler, and he was a professor at the City of London College. It was the first significant lead they had in their search for Amara's mother.

It was getting late, and both Henry and Amara were feeling tired. They said goodbye to Arthur and returned to Henry's flat to update his mother and get some rest before continuing the search the next day.

When they arrived, Mary was patiently waiting at the kitchen table with a cup of peppermint tea. They sat down, showed her the diaries, and explained everything they had discovered that day. They talked for a couple of hours before heading to bed. Amara went to Henry's room while he took the sofa.

That night, Amara went to bed feeling a little happier. What if she found her mother the next day? The thought filled her with so much excitement that she couldn't sleep. Suddenly, there was a knock at the door.

"Hey, can I come in?" Henry asked, poking his head in.

"Of course, come on in."

As he stepped inside, Henry noticed she was fidgeting. He asked her how she was feeling. Amara admitted that she was excited about the progress they had made and hopeful about finding her mother, but she also felt nervous about meeting her and scared of facing Agnes.

"You know what always makes me feel better and it's my favourite event of the year in Gulrose?"

"No, what is it?" Henry raised his left eyebrow.

"The Queen's and King's Ball. It happens every year to honour the royal family in the kingdom. I always get all dressed up and dance," she said with a smile, though a small frown tugged at her lips.

Henry smiled, stood up, and put on a slow song. He walked over to her, bowed, and, holding out his hand, asked her to dance. She smiled, nervously tucked her hair behind her ear, and stood up.

They began to slow dance, their smiles soft as they gazed into each other's eyes. Henry had always known Amara's eyes were beautiful, but he had never realised how easily one could get lost in them. For the first time, his mind was quiet, free of the constant overthinking that usually filled his thoughts.

He slowly spun her around, prompting a soft chuckle from her. She rested her head on his chest and closed her eyes, their thumbs tracing gentle patterns as if performing their own little dance. Even though music played in the background, their minds felt completely silent, as if time itself had stopped. Henry placed his left hand on Amara's cheek, his gaze fixed on her. He leaned in closer, their breaths mingling, until their lips met in a soft, fleeting kiss. Amara opened her eyes for a moment, then closed them again. The kiss was short, sweet, and tender, leaving a tingling sensation coursing through her.

They exchanged smiles before resuming their dance for a while longer, neither wanting the moment to end. Eventually, they sat down, exhausted but unwilling to sleep—they wanted to savour every second together.

Amara shared stories from her childhood, explaining how growing up without her mother had shaped her and affected her relationship with her father. Henry listened, understanding all too well. He had grown up without a father figure, and it had left its mark on him too. While he deeply loved his mother, who had always been there for him, there were things he couldn't share with her.

Whether it was the excitement of the day or the sudden change in their feelings, they both knew one thing for certain: this was just the beginning of their story together. Though they didn't yet know what their future held, if asked at that moment, they would both picture it as bright—a future full of promise once they overcame the challenges ahead.

If only they knew how much heartbreak, death, darkness, and betrayal awaited them along the way

CHAPTER 4

Finding Catherine

In the morning, they all woke up early and went to see Professor Moler. When they arrived, they were greeted by a less-than-enthusiastic receptionist.

They explained who they were looking for, hoping she would help them.

"Please wait here," she said in a monotone voice.

After a while on the phone, she informed them that Professor Moler was in his office and that they could go in. She pointed in the direction of his office and then turned her back to them.

When they knocked on his door, a deep voice from inside told them to come in. Upon opening the door, they saw a tall man in his mid-thirties.

"Hello, gentlemen. How can I help you?" asked Nicholas.

Henry and Arthur exchanged glances. Nicholas couldn't see Amara, so they knew he didn't believe.

"Hi, my name is Henry, and this is Arthur. We would like to ask if you happen to know someone named Catherine. We believe you've met her, and we need to find her."

Nicholas's facial expression changed, and his smile faded, as though he knew exactly who they were talking about without needing much clarification.

They explained further, telling him that Catherine's daughter was looking for her, and it would be a big help if he could tell them where they might find her.

Nicholas didn't seem eager to help them, but in the end, he provided all the information he knew so they would leave.

"This is the last address I have for her," he said, writing it down on a piece of paper.

"But be careful; you cannot trust that woman," he added cautiously before handing the paper over.

"Why not?" asked Henry.

But Nicholas didn't want to discuss it any further and sent them on their way, being rather rude at the end of their encounter.

When they left, they were pleased with the outcome of their visit but also concerned. What did he mean when he said not to trust Catherine? What had happened between them? What had she done to him?

When the group arrived at the address, they stood outside for a while. Amara hesitated to walk in. If her mother was, in fact, there, they would have so much to talk about. She couldn't wait to see her.

She had only ever seen one photograph of her mother, which she had taken from her father's room. Her mother was beautiful, with long dark brown hair and green-blue eyes. Her smile was so bright it could light up an entire room.

Henry saw Amara fidgeting and cracking her knuckles. He gently grabbed her hand and smiled.

"Everything is going to be okay. I am here with you all the way, I promise."

Amara smiled, took a deep breath, and knocked on the door. When it opened, there she was—her mother. Amara's expression shifted from anticipation to shock in an instant, and soon tears were streaming down her cheeks. Catherine recognised her daughter immediately; she looked just like her, except for the eyes. Catherine launched at Amara and hugged her tightly. They embraced for what felt like forever, as if it were just the two of them there. When they finally separated, Catherine invited them in.

She made them all tea, and after brief introductions, she explained what had happened when she arrived in this world. She didn't know where to look for the pendant, was scared, and had nowhere to sleep. After days of roaming the streets, she went to a library to get warm, and it was there that she befriended Nicholas.

They became quite close very quickly. Catherine told him who and what she was looking for, but she didn't share the whole story—she didn't think he would believe her anyway. Nicholas liked Catherine. Like many men before him, he was infatuated with her beauty. It took almost a year, but after some research, he was able to help her find Ann. For Catherine, that was the end of the story between them, and all she had to do was wait for her daughter to hopefully find her.

However, for Nicholas, that wasn't the end of their relationship.

It seemed he wanted more than just friendship with Catherine, and when she denied his advances, he felt that she had only been using him to help her find Ann. That wasn't her intention, of course, but she couldn't afford to befriend anyone in this world; it could put them in danger. So, she left and never spoke to him again.

She found a job at a little boutique, secured a place to live, and waited. She waited for seventeen years, remaining in one place to allow Amara to find her.

Theodore had sent her a message that Amara was finally coming to find her, and he hoped Catherine would be able to locate the pendant. She wished she could send a message back to him and remembered it was the only time she had wished she were a witch. At least then, Amara would know where to look for her or could have come to her sooner. For Catherine, it had been torture to be apart from her daughter all this time.

Now it all made sense to them why Nicholas had said what he did earlier. He was resentful towards Catherine because she didn't want to be with him.

"Mother, I'm so glad I found you! But how do we get back to Gulrose?"

"You will take us there, darling."

Catherine explained that before Theodore had sent her to this land, he had given her a spell that would bring them back once Amara found her. She had guarded it all this time. All Amara had to do was read it aloud and concentrate on their home. She had enough power to take them all back.

Amara felt nervous. The only time she had used her powers for something significant was by accident— when she got angry or scared. She had never used them on purpose and didn't know how. She had only ever performed small spells that Theodore had taught her.

Catherine believed in her daughter and knew she could bring them back.

"Thank you both, by the way, for helping Amara on her journey," said Catherine to Henry and Arthur.

They both smiled, and Henry asked Amara if he could speak to her alone. They went into the other room, where Henry asked.

"Do you think my mum and I could come with you?"

"You would want to?" her eyebrows raised.

"Yes. It's where we're from, and I don't want to lose you," he said, looking down, biting his lower lip.

Amara smiled and gently touched his hand. They sat in silence for a while, just the two of them. For the first time since she met him, Amara felt something for Henry that she hadn't felt before. She didn't want to lose him either. She hugged him tightly and said she would love for both of them to come back home with her. After a moment of quiet reflection, they decided to return to Catherine.

When they came back out, they told her their plan for Henry and Mary to join them. Henry explained that his mother had revealed the truth about his origins, and he wanted to see his real home and learn more about his father.

Catherine agreed, but everyone could see on her face that she wasn't entirely happy about this decision. But why? No one knew. Not yet.

They realised they had to leave soon; it wasn't safe here with a hunter on their trail. Catherine instructed Henry to go and gather his mother and his belongings.

Once Henry left, Amara talked a bit more with Catherine. She shared how her father had always discouraged her from embracing her powers, shielding her from everything and everyone.

He never even spoke about Catherine. Everything Amara learned about her mother came later, when Theodore finally explained what had happened all those years ago. He used to tell her stories about witches and manticores, how being a shapeshifter ran in their family. Amara didn't know if she had that ability; her father wasn't much help. He didn't spend a lot of time with her, so she never learned to transform.

Meanwhile, Henry returned to his flat. Just as he was about to take out his keys, he noticed that the door was slightly ajar. He stepped inside and was met with an eerie silence. As he walked through the flat, calling for his mother, he caught sight of her at the far end of the kitchen. She was sitting on the floor, her back against the cabinets.

"Mum! What's happened?" he shouted, rushing to her side and kneeling next to her.

"He came here," she gasped, her voice trembling. "He was looking for her. The hunter!"

"I'm so sorry, Mum. I shouldn't have left you here," Henry cried, guilt flooding over him.

Mary looked up at her son, her expression a mix of fear and relief. "It's not your fault. I should have come with you. I shouldn't have let you and Amara leave on your own. Where is she? Is she safe? I didn't tell him anything."

"Yes, she's safe. I came back for you. We'll go back. We'll go back to Gulrose, Mum. You have to come quickly."

Mary wanted to go back, despite having run away from there long ago. But she carried a secret she had never shared with Henry—or anyone else—and if they returned, he would learn the truth. She noticed how he looked at Amara, and she knew he would go no matter what. Reluctantly, she decided she must accompany him, to ensure both her son and her secret remained safe.

Henry gently helped his mother clean the blood from her face, his hands trembling slightly, and together, they made their way back to Catherine's flat. As they arrived, he noticed the charged looks exchanged between Catherine and Mary. It was clear they recognised each other, and an undercurrent of tension suggested there was unresolved conflict between them. Yet Henry pushed his concerns aside; he knew Amara needed him now, and they didn't have time for distractions.

They all gathered around the pendant, and Catherine

handed Amara the spell that would transport them back.

Amara studied the words, her heart racing as she took a deep breath. Doubts clouded her mind—would she be able to bring everyone back? Would the spell even work? But she also felt the weight of responsibility; every single person in that room was counting on her.

The pressure got the better of her, and she started to doubt herself. She believed she wasn't as strong as everyone always said she was.

Henry stood next to her and held her hand.

"You can do this; I know you can. You just have to believe in yourself, like I believe in you," he told her.

Amara smiled, grabbed the pendant with her other hand, and began chanting the spell.

"Ta mig härifrån, ta mig härifrån."

Everyone had their eyes shut for a while, but nothing happened.

Amara stopped chanting and said, "See, I can't do this. I don't know how. It just doesn't work."

"Yes, you can. You can do more than you think you can. Believe in yourself and your strength. Think of our home," Catherine pleaded.

Amara closed her eyes again. This time, she thought of her home. She pictured the beautiful yellow roses that grew in her garden, and she thought of her people. They needed her. She had to make it back to them and defeat Agnes.

She started chanting again. She felt power flowing through her veins. This was the first time she could feel it like this. It was getting stronger and stronger, surprising her.

She was a bit scared by the feeling, but she also liked it. After a few seconds, a bright light burst from the pendant. A window in Catherine's apartment flew open, and a strong wind blew into the room from nowhere. Amara chanted louder and louder until, suddenly, there was silence.

When she opened her eyes, she was still holding Henry's hand. She looked around and saw her mother, Mary, and Arthur. They were back in the Gulrose Kingdom, and they were safe.

Amara fell to her knees. This spell was incredibly powerful, and it had exhausted her. Henry knelt beside her and hugged her. She looked up and saw a beautiful, clear blue sky. She smelled the fresh air she remembered and felt happy to be home.

Catherine looked around, hardly able to believe she was home. The place hadn't changed at all—it was still as beautiful as she remembered. Yet, even though she was happy to be back, she also felt nervous. Suddenly, she realised she would have to face her husband.

The King didn't know she was still alive; he believed she had died, just as she had planned with Theodore. She had never told him about Agnes, the potion, the pendant, or that she'd had to leave to protect their daughter. Now, she knew she would have to tell him everything, and she wasn't sure if he would ever forgive her for deceiving him in this way. Amara walked up to her mother and held her hand.

They were standing in a large field, gazing at the beautiful castle. Both of them wanted nothing more than to run towards it, but they knew they couldn't—not yet. They didn't have time to explain what had happened or to face all the people waiting. First, they needed to hide and figure out how to defeat Agnes.

As they stood there, simply taking in the view, an arrow suddenly flew past Catherine's ear, narrowly missing her.

"RUN!" screamed Henry as he rushed toward them. "RUUUN!"

They all sprinted into the woods, closely pursued by a hunter—a tall man dressed in brown. A quiver full of arrows hung on his back, as he gripped a bow in his hand. He had found them, and it was clear he wouldn't give up without a fight. They were sure he would stop at nothing, willing to kill them all if it meant bringing Amara to Agnes.

After what felt like hours, they finally stopped running, only when they believed they'd lost him. They found themselves deep in the woods. It was getting dark, and they knew they would have to camp out for the night.

Henry and Arthur began to search the area, armed with nothing but a few wooden sticks. Although Henry wouldn't admit it—wanting to impress Amara—he was terrified they might run into the hunter again, knowing he couldn't really defend himself.

Meanwhile, Catherine, Mary, and Amara stayed behind, working to make a fire and some shelter for the night. After a while, Henry and Arthur returned, relieved to report they hadn't found any sign of the hunter nearby.

It seemed they had truly lost him, but they knew it was only a matter of time before he found them again. He was from this land and most likely knew his way around the forest. They were actually a bit surprised they had managed to lose him so easily, and it made them slightly suspicious.

After finding a spot that seemed comfortable enough, they decided they would rest there for a few hours and be on the move again as soon as the sun rose.

CHAPTER 5

The Art Of Witchcraft

When Amara woke up, she realised she had never felt more exhausted than she did right then, but there was no time to rest.

She needed to venture further into the Dark Forest, find Agnes, and, with any luck, put an end to all of this. Once she succeeded, she and her mother could return to the castle and finally be happy together. They could be a family again.

Henry could hardly believe his eyes. This was the place where he was born, but of course, he didn't recognise any of it. He had been only a baby when his mother took him and fled. He sensed a strange breeze in the air; it was so different from London, it smelled different.

Somehow, he could almost swear he remembered the scent. He glanced down at his feet, noticing the grass beneath him—a strange shade of green, almost as if it were alive, like something out of a drawing.

Now that they had a long journey ahead, he felt he needed answers about why they had left. He ran up to his mother and fell into step beside her.

"Mum, can you tell me the truth about why you took me away from here? Why did we run?" Henry asked.

Mary didn't want to reveal the real reason behind their escape, but she knew, now that they were back, she had to. She told Henry that when his father was killed, everyone believed that Henry's uncle—his father's own brother—was behind the murder. She had been terrified that Henry and she would be next, especially with no one left to protect them. Fearful for their lives, she took Henry and fled. She had no idea where they could go; she knew nowhere in or around Gulrose would be safe.

Desperate, she went to Theodore and begged him to help them, and he agreed. He promised to find a safe place for them to hide. He had once heard of a land far from the kingdom, a place where magic didn't exist. He found a spell that would allow him to send them there—to London—where no one would ever find them.

Henry felt a mix of anger and understanding. He was upset to have learned the truth so late, but he understood why his mother had done what she did. She had risked everything to protect him, and now that they were back, he knew it was his turn to protect her—and Amara.

Ah, Amara. Strong feelings stirred within him every time he thought of her. He was smitten.

Mary, noticing how often he looked at or mentioned Amara, finally said, "You can't be together, you know. You and Amara."

Henry looked at her, confused. "Why not?" he asked.

"You just can't, please just trust me on this."

Henry didn't say another word. He knew they had bigger things to worry about. Instead, he turned and looked at Amara. When she caught him watching her, she smiled, and he felt his heart skip a beat.

He ran back to her.

"Happy birthday, by the way."

She chuckled. "How did you know?"

"Well, your mum told me." He smiled.

"I used to love my birthday, you know. I'd spend the day with people in the kingdom, getting to know them and their lives."

Henry smiled, admiring her kindness and the way she genuinely cared for her people.

They walked for a few more hours until Catherine stopped them. She knew exactly where Agnes lived, and she knew they were very close. To stand a chance, they had to catch Agnes off guard. Hopefully, she wasn't yet aware they were here, and they could use the element of surprise. Their plan was to ambush her, allowing Amara to use the pendant to end this—if it would work.

They knew it wouldn't be easy, but they had to try. They would do whatever it took to stop Agnes and protect Amara.

They slowly sneaked up on her house and looked through the window. She was there, sitting in her chair, reading one of her grimoires.

Henry was surprised; he had imagined an old, ugly woman, as most would when thinking of an "evil witch," but Agnes wasn't that at all. She was of average height, slender, with long, straight dark hair. She looked well-groomed, even elegant, and strikingly attractive for her age.

Amara took off the pendant and held it tightly in her hand. Doubts filled her mind. She'd never been able to practice this spell—she had only one chance. One shot at freedom.

Henry leaned towards her and whispered, "You've got this. Just breathe. On three, get ready. One, two, three."

He swung the door open, and Amara stepped inside. She looked at Agnes, her heart pounding, her hands trembling. But she forced herself to be brave.

"You will not have me," she said, her voice steadying as she began to chant the spell her mother had given her upon their arrival. The spell meant to trap Agnes's power.

"Ström in innesluta, Ström in innesluta."

A strong wind filled the air, and the pendant started to glow. Amara kept chanting, feeling more powerful with every word. The wind grew stronger, swirling around her, as the pendant's light intensified.

Henry, Arthur, Catherine, and Mary stood there, watching. They were certain Agnes's powers would soon be trapped. The air was thick with tension, and as the wind peaked in strength, it suddenly died down. The pendant's glow faded abruptly.

Amara looked down at the pendant in confusion. Had she captured Agnes's power? Nothing else seemed to happen. And then, she heard it—a cold, mocking laugh that sent chills down her spine, a sound they would all remember long after this night.

"You really thought it would be this easy? That you could just come in here and defeat me? You silly little girl. You could be so much more powerful, but you're too stubborn, just like your mother," said Agnes while looking at Catherine with disgust.

Amara looked terrified. Agnes waved her hand, and suddenly, everyone—Henry, Arthur, Catherine, and Mary—disappeared, leaving Amara alone. The others reappeared on the far side of the woods, utterly disoriented.

Now it was just the two of them. Alone in the dim, shadowy cottage. Agnes came closer to Amara who was breathing heavily, her heart beating intensely inside her chest.

"Come, little one, we have a lot to talk about," Agnes said with a creepy smile on her face.

Amara didn't want to talk to her; she wanted to go home and be with her family without worrying every second of her life. She wanted to know where Agnes had sent them and if they were all safe.

Agnes wanted to be nice to Amara. She wanted to show her that they could live together peacefully, but patience wasn't one of her strengths.

"I said, sit," shouted Agnes, and with another wave of her hand, she made Amara sit in her ugly purple armchair.

"Why didn't it work? The pendant. Is it because of me?"

Agnes started making them some tea and said, "It doesn't work because it's a fake."

Agnes had made this replica and stolen the real pendant from London as soon as she heard about its whereabouts eighteen years ago. She crafted it so that it still had some magic in it and could be used to cast spells, but it did not have the same power as the original. It wouldn't be able to absorb a witch's magic. Unfortunately, magic like that was not available to Agnes or anyone, for that matter. The spell that created this very special pendant was long gone. Lost. No one could ever find it. Agnes knew the real pendant could take away her powers, and her dream of having a new coven of witches in the Gulrose Kingdom would never come true.

She couldn't risk anyone finding it and using it against her. Amara was confused. That meant Agnes had the real pendant this whole time. Her mother never had to leave her and live alone in that strange place for all those years. Her mother had risked her life to find the pendant. They had been separated, and Amara had grown up without her, believing she had died. She felt broken her whole life, as if a part of her heart was missing.

She couldn't believe that everything they had both gone through was for nothing. And now it was too late. She couldn't defeat Agnes without the pendant, and she was trapped there with her.

Before she could think of anything else or ask any more questions, the door swung open. A man dressed entirely in brown stood there—the hunter.

"Finally," said Agnes, clearly annoyed with him.

Amara had only seen him briefly twice before: first when he was chasing her and Henry in London, and again when he pursued them after shooting an arrow at her mother, but she had never seen his face properly.

He had blond curly hair, blue eyes, and was quite tall, very handsome. She knew he was evil, but she couldn't stop looking at him. She quickly came to her senses and turned around so she wouldn't have to face him.

"Well, she is here, isn't she? So, what does it matter?" he finally said. His voice was deep.

"It matters because it was your job to bring her here, and you couldn't even do that. I am very disappointed in you. What had I trained you for all these years?"

"Fine, Mother. You win, as always," he said snappishly.

"By the way, you threw me against the wall. Nice, very tempting," he winked at Amara.

She was dumbfounded. The hunter was Agnes's son, and now she was there with both of them, not knowing what would happen. What did they plan to do to her?

Meanwhile, Henry knew he had to get back to Amara, but they were on the other side of the woods. It would take them at least a whole day to get back there, and without the pendant and Amara by their side, they didn't stand a chance against the witch.

Henry was beside himself. He couldn't bear being without Amara, not knowing if she was safe or if she was hurt.

Then Catherine had an idea. If they could get into the castle unnoticed and find Theodore, maybe he could help them. He had a lot of knowledge about the pendant, Amara, and witches in general. Perhaps there was another way they could defeat her that he hadn't thought of before. It wasn't a perfect plan, but he was the only one they had.

They were tired and hungry, so they turned around and started walking towards the castle, which was only an hour away from where they were. Catherine felt her chest tightening; her anxiety was getting worse.

When they arrived, they ran alongside the wall and slipped past the knights guarding the back of the castle. Catherine still remembered her way around. There were tunnels underneath that had been used in olden times when humans were at war with witches and someone from the castle needed a quick escape.

They entered Theodore's chambers and shut the door behind them. Theodore was reading a book in his favourite chair, smoking a pipe. He looked up, startled, and couldn't believe his eyes. Catherine was right there, she was back. He stood up and walked over to her. They hugged as Catherine sobbed, overwhelmed with anger, sadness, and fear. She let herself be vulnerable around him. Theodore had always been like a father to Catherine, and he thought of her as a daughter. They had a very close relationship, and he always felt the need to protect her.

He quickly realised that if Catherine was there, then Amara should be as well. He saw Mary standing behind her. Mary also hugged him and thanked him for all the help and the messages he had sent. She introduced her son and Arthur to him.

Henry couldn't shake the feeling that he knew Theodore, and then it struck him. He had been having strange dreams for weeks now. In the dreams, Henry was running, but he didn't know from what or whom.

He just knew he was petrified of something or someone. He ran and ran when suddenly he fell, and when he tried to get up, an old man was there to help him. The man always said the same sentence before Henry woke up:

"She will be the doom for us all."

His thoughts were interrupted by Catherine, who started to explain everything to Theodore as quickly as she could. When she finished, she pleaded with him to help them. There had to be something else they could do.

"I wish I could help you, Catherine, but the pendant was the only thing that could defeat her," he said.

"Maybe we don't have to defeat her—not yet anyway. We might just need to find something to help us retrieve Amara and the pendant and try to absorb her power again," said Henry.

This gave Theodore an idea. He began to go through his books and finally found the one he was looking for. This book told the legend of a very dark wizard from a long time ago. He was so powerful that no one could defeat him. Another wizard had imprisoned him for a time with a spell, giving people a chance to escape his wrath.

This spell wouldn't hold for long if you weren't strong enough, but it would work for a little while. Theodore might have enough power to perform this spell on Agnes, while the others rescued Amara and retrieved the pendant. However, they would have to be quick. He wasn't sure if he could even perform the spell or how long he would be able to maintain it.

It was decided that Mary would stay behind, as she still wasn't healed from the attack by the hunter in London. She would go to an old friend who lived nearby to recover. After they said their goodbyes, the rest set off on their journey to retrieve Amara.

CHAPTER 6

Betrayal

Amara was sitting down, looking up at Agnes.

"What do you want with me?" she asked.

Agnes looked concerned and replied, "I am not going to hurt you, Amara. Together, you, Aiden, and I will rebuild what was once lost—what your grandfather took from us."

Amara knew exactly what this meant. She would be stuck with Agnes and her son, and they would use her powers to incite an uprising.

Agnes prepared a meal and offered Amara a change of clothes. They all sat down to eat dinner—well, the two of them did, but Amara didn't eat; she just kept watching them, trying to figure out how to escape by looking around the cottage's windows and doors.

After they finished dinner, Agnes showed Amara to her room. In her mind, they had a lot of work to do, and they needed to start soon.

Word had already spread that Amara was here, and very soon all the witches who had fled Gulrose years ago would return, and they would once again be in power. No one would be able to stop them.

Before Agnes left Amara by herself, she said, "And don't try to escape. I have the whole cottage under a protection spell. Goodnight."

Amara couldn't sleep that night. All she could think about was her future here if she didn't escape. But how could she? The spell wouldn't allow her to leave, and she didn't know how to break it. She tried to leave many times, but whatever exit she attempted, the spell wouldn't allow her. She was trapped and desperate. She didn't know they were all coming back for her. It would take them hours to reach Agnes's cottage, as they had to cross the entire Dark Forest.

When Amara woke up in the morning, Agnes wanted to start training right away.
They went outside the cottage and practised spells in the morning, with Aiden just watching them and

not doing anything. Amara wasn't very good at the spells Agnes was trying to teach her. She kept failing at everything she attempted. It wasn't that she couldn't do it; she just wasn't trying hard enough. She didn't want to. She didn't want to do anything that would help them.

Aiden saw this and noticed how frustrated his mother was. Suddenly, he stood up and, using his powers, hurled a large log at Amara. Before she could even think, she placed her hand in front of her face and stopped it.

"Are you crazy? Why would you do that?" Amara asked as the log hit the ground.

Aiden smirked and sat back down. "To prove a point. You're not getting better on purpose."

"See? You have the power, and we need it. Please," Agnes said.

Amara didn't respond. Agnes looked at her. "I promise you; we don't want to hurt anyone. We just want our family back, and you are the key to that.

Please, just try to help us. We don't want all that power to fight, but we need it to protect ourselves."

Amara knew she shouldn't trust either of them, but she couldn't help but notice the desperation in Agnes's eyes.

These two were all alone, wanting to reunite their family. How was it any different from when Amara was trying to find her mother and bring her family back together?

This was one of Amara's greatest strengths, but sometimes also her biggest weakness: her compassion and how deeply she felt other people's pain. At that moment, she didn't like it, because it made her consider, for just a moment, helping them.

When the training was over, Amara sat outside. She thought about her mother, the castle, her people, but mostly, Henry. She missed him.

As she thought about how much he had helped her and how happy she felt whenever he was near, she couldn't help but wish he were there with her now.

She walked around the cottage and noticed a bush of yellow roses blooming behind it. A smile crept onto her face; yellow roses had been her favourite flower since childhood. Kneeling down, she inhaled their sweet fragrance and closed her eyes, allowing memories of her youth to wash over her. Though she didn't have many happy memories, the scent of roses always brought back the cherished moments with Theodore, who would read to her from his books.

She recalled running around the garden while Theodore chased her, their laughter ringing through the air. She remembered sitting beneath the tall tree in their backyard, captivated as he shared tales of mythical creatures. He had always been there for her, filling her life with love—something her father had never done.

A single tear slipped down her cheek as she realised just how much she had loved him. Then another tear followed, and soon there were more.

"Am I interrupting something?" Aiden approached her, breaking the spell of her memories.

"Yes, actually, you are," Amara replied coldly, quickly wiping away her tears.

He looked disheartened but sat down beside her anyway.

"Look, I know you don't want to be here, and I can't blame you. But we really need your help."

Amara looked at him, and her facial expression changed.

"I know. I understand you need my help; I just don't like the way you and your mother treat the people around me to get it. You almost killed my mum, Aiden."

"But I didn't, and I never miss," he said.

"What do you mean?" She looked confused.

"I never miss my target."

Amara watched him walk away. It made her think. If Aiden never missed, how had he missed her mum yesterday? Did this mean he had done it on purpose? Maybe he didn't want to hurt her mother and her friends; he just wanted to find her so she could help them unite their family.

She couldn't help but feel sorry for both of them. Maybe she could help them, and after all was done, she could go back to her family and back to Henry. Perhaps she could negotiate her own terms with them.

Amara gathered her courage and walked over to Agnes.

"If I help you, I will set the rules."

Agnes closed her book and took off her glasses. "I am listening."

"No one will get hurt — my family and friends. Everyone will be safe, and after we are done, and you have your family back, I will go back to mine."

Agnes looked over at Aiden, then back at Amara, and smiled. "That sounds reasonable, but I would like to negotiate my own terms."

Amara took a deep breath. "Fine."

"I agree that your family and friends will not be harmed, but you will stay longer with us. I need you to stay not just until we reunite the coven, but for a bit longer, to give them hope again. To make them believe in me, in us."

"What do you mean by 'a bit longer'? How long?"

"Shall we say a year?" asked Agnes.

Amara sighed and thought about it for a moment. She didn't want to stay for a year, but what was the alternative? Her family and Henry could die. She felt like she had no choice.

Agnes would keep her anyway; she would not let her leave. Amara knew this was the best deal she could get, so she agreed.

"Fine, I will stay for a year."

Agnes motioned to Amara to go outside. They stepped in front of the cottage and began to work on her spells again. This time, she was doing much better because she wanted to.

Well, at least she wanted to try a little bit, instead of just refusing as she had before. She wanted to do well so all of this could be over. She didn't know half of the horror that the year she had promised to Agnes would bring.

Henry was getting more and more nervous as they approached the cottage. Catherine could see how worried he was, so she approached him.

"We will save her, Henry, and she will be with us soon, I promise."

"I really care about your daughter, and I want her to be safe and happy."

"I know you do, and I can tell she also cares about you very much," she replied.

Henry felt pleased. He knew he and Amara had grown close, but he didn't know if she felt the same way he did. Now, her own mother was telling him she did. Who knows a daughter better than her own mother, even though they had been apart for a long time? This motivated him even more to go and get her. Once they did, maybe they could be together. It gave him a different type of strength. He was still scared, but now he was ready. He was ready to fight whatever or whoever might come between them, no matter the danger he might face. He was so happy that he didn't notice Catherine's face. She looked troubled and worried when she spoke of him and Amara.

As they were all walking, Henry suddenly stopped. He began looking all around him, listening intently. Everyone else stopped as well, but they didn't know why; they couldn't hear or see anything.

"What is it?" asked Theodore. "What do you see?"

"I don't see anything, but I hear something. Something is coming," replied Henry. He didn't understand how he was the only one who could hear the noise. It sounded like wings—lots of them.

Before he could warn the others, a flock of ravens came at them, clawing and attacking. Henry picked up a branch lying nearby and tried to hit as many of them as he could, especially the ones attacking Catherine; she seemed to be the main target. Arthur and Theodore did the same, and after they got rid of most of the ravens, they all started to run.

They fled deeper into the woods and hid under a small mountain opening. They waited there for a while to ensure the ravens were gone.

They knew this wasn't a coincidence. Someone had sent the ravens to scare them off—or worse, to seriously harm them. They suspected it had to be Agnes. Somehow, she knew they were coming to get Amara.

The sun was going down again; it was getting dark. They had to set up yet another camp and stay there for the night. Henry decided to take the first watch. They didn't want to be surprised by another attack, and they also didn't know what kind of animals lived in these woods.

Everyone tried to get as comfortable as they could, and Henry sat down near the fire, trying to warm up. After a while, everyone fell asleep.

Henry struggled to stay awake. He stood up, stretched his legs, and walked around a little bit. All he could think about was whether they would be successful in saving Amara.

When everyone woke up in the morning, he was exhausted. He had been up the whole night, but he knew he had to try to gather as much strength as he could, as they still had a long journey ahead of them.

It took them another half a day to walk all the way across the forest to Agnes' house.

As they stood a bit further away, trying to figure out how to get inside quickly and hopefully freeze Agnes, they suddenly saw Amara walking out of the house. She knelt in front of a dead flower, staring at it. Then she put her hands around it, closed her eyes, and began to whisper. The flower started to bloom, but not fully. Amara grew frustrated but tried again. This time, Aiden walked out of the house and placed his hand on her shoulder. Amara looked up and smiled, then turned her attention back to the flower. She began to chant again, and this time the flower bloomed fully. She chuckled and stood up. Aiden knelt next to the flower, picked it up.

He looked at Amara, smiled, and tucked the flower behind her ear. They both just stood there, smiling and looking at each other.

The group was confused. What was happening? Were they now friends? Was Amara under some kind of spell? Who was this boy?

Henry felt like his heart shattered into a million pieces. He didn't want to believe that what he had just seen was real, so he decided the only explanation was that Amara was indeed under Agnes' and Aiden's spell.

She and Aiden went back inside, and Agnes stepped out. She was standing in front of her house, breathing in the fresh air. This was their chance. She was there, alone.

They all ran out, armed, while Theodore began to walk towards Agnes as he chanted a spell.

"Frysa på plats, Frysa på plats, Frysa på plats,"

Agnes stood there, shocked that they had made it this far; she hadn't expected them to show up after she sent the ravens. She tried to cast a protective spell, but it was too late; she slowly froze in place. It was working, and now they had a chance to rescue Amara. They noticed she had the pendant around her neck, although they didn't realise it was a fake. Their excitement didn't last long, however.

"Stop!" shouted Amara. She stood outside the house, Aiden by her side. Confusion spread across everyone's faces, but Theodore didn't stop; he kept chanting and moving closer to Agnes, his hand shaking.

"She said stop, old man!" shouted Aiden as he advanced towards Theodore, his hand raised in warning.

"Sätta i halsen, sätta i halsen, sätta i halsen."

Theodore suddenly stopped. He could feel his throat closing up, not being able to speak.

Agnes was free; she fell to her knees, and Amara rushed to her side. She picked her up, checking to see if she was alright. Then she turned to Aiden and said, "Leave him."

Aiden complied, and Theodore was released from the spell. Amara then ran to him, checking to see if he was alright as well. She looked into his eyes, touched his hand and whispered.

"I am sorry. I had no choice."

CHAPTER 7

Reunion

"Why are you doing this? We came here to save you, Amara," said Catherine.

She looked at her mother, walked up to her, and smiled. "I know you did, Mother. But I need to help them. They only want to reunite their family, just as we do, and once that's done, I will come back to you unharmed. I promise. A year. We agreed on a year."

"A year?" Henry interrupted their conversation. "So what? If we hadn't come here, would you just not have told us? You wouldn't have said goodbye?"

Amara looked at him, grabbed his hand, and led him a little further from everyone else. She wanted to speak to him alone.

"I am sorry; I had no choice. It was either this deal or something much worse. I had to do it to protect all of you."

"We could help you. We almost had the pendant," said Henry.

"The pendant around her neck is a fake, Henry. She made it, and she's had the real one this whole time."

Henry's facial expression changed from emotionless to one of slight shock, his mouth slightly open. This meant their plan would never work anyway. He understood now why Amara did what she did.

"Fine, but I still don't understand. We could have come up with a different plan. We would have."

"No, no you wouldn't. Don't you get it? She's too powerful, and so is he. This is what's best for everyone."

Henry clenched his jaw but didn't say a word. He knew there was no convincing Amara that this was a bad idea.

They went back to the group so Amara could say her goodbyes. When they returned to everyone, Amara walked up to Catherine, who put her hand on her cheek.

She understood, and even though she didn't agree, she was proud of who her daughter had become: a compassionate future queen with a kind heart. That was what their people needed.

Amara promised that she would let them know every day that she was safe, and she would keep them updated on the progress she made. Agnes' ravens would carry the letters to them.

They said their goodbyes, cried, hugged, and went their separate ways. Amara went back to Agnes and Aiden, and the rest went on their way back to the castle. All of them walked slowly with their heads down, clearly feeling as though they had failed.

Suddenly, Catherine was overcome with a torrent of emotions. Her hands started to shake, cold sweat ran down her back, and her stomach felt like it was in a knot. She hadn't seen her husband since she had faked her own death, and now she was supposed to come back as if no time had passed. She wasn't sure if he would forgive her or if she would be able to stay in the castle.

Henry couldn't shake the feeling that Amara wasn't safe there, especially with Aiden around. He didn't trust him and wasn't sure how he would treat her.

The thought of Aiden being near her while he couldn't, was infuriating.

When they arrived in front of the castle, the guards, of course, didn't recognise Catherine, and she couldn't just tell them she was the Queen of Gulrose Kingdom.

Instead, they were led inside to wait for the king, with the guards standing with their hands ready on their swords. It took a while for him to arrive, and Catherine grew more and more nervous.

Then she heard heavy footsteps. From behind a corner, a tall figure appeared, and there he was, as handsome as she remembered. The king stopped in the middle of the hall, looking as if he had just seen a ghost. Of course, that's what he thought it was; his wife had died. She had died 17 years ago, so that was the only explanation in his mind.

"Hello, William," said Catherine simply.

"C-Catherine, is that really you? How is this even possible?" His jaw dropped. "And who are these people?" William asked, referencing Henry and Arthur, as he, of course, knew Theodore.

Catherine came closer and put her hands on his face. She promised that she would explain everything, but first, she introduced Henry and Arthur. Then the two of them went into a private room where Catherine told William everything. She explained how she had faked her own death to go and find the pendant that would save their daughter, where Amara had disappeared to, what was happening with her now, and the deal she had made with the witch—everything.

William couldn't believe what he was hearing. He didn't know how to feel: relieved? Angry? He was glad she was alive and well, but he felt betrayed—so betrayed, in fact, that he didn't think he could forgive her, at least not for now. She could, of course, stay in the castle, but they would occupy separate rooms, and her return would not be shared among the people of the kingdom for the time being. He was a very proud man and felt that his Queen's return and the real story would make him look like a fool.

Catherine was devastated. She knew he would be angry with her, but she hadn't expected him to react this way. She was exhausted after all the travel, so she arranged for Henry and Arthur to each have a room and went into her new chambers. Henry's room was down the hall from Theodore's, and Arthur's was next to Henry's. The three of them grew very close, very quickly. They would exchange knowledge from their own worlds. Henry wanted to know more about the kingdom, and Theodore was fascinated by London.

They spent their nights talking about both places and how Henry wanted to learn how to fight. He had always admired knights, and now that he was back where he was born, and they were, in fact, real, maybe he could become one. But that wasn't the only reason. He knew he would come face to face with Aiden again, probably soon, and he needed to be able to beat him in a fight. He wanted to learn how to shoot an arrow, how to use a sword, ride a horse, and everything else he could.

He liked the palace and the surroundings. He loved the garden, which was full of yellow roses. He remembered a story Amara had told him back in London. Whenever she felt alone, scared, or just bored, she would go into their garden and sit down next to the bush of yellow roses. She would read different books and could just be herself. She would practice small spells when her father wasn't looking and read about all the different types of magic. So, he did the same; he would sit in the garden next to the roses. He would read history books and books on knights. It made him feel closer to her, as if she would come home any minute.

He knew he would be happy here once she was back with him and they could be together.

Henry asked Theodore to teach him everything about witches, manticores and their history. Theodore was somewhat of an expert on all of this; he had read every book on the history of mystical creatures they had in the kingdom's library, which was very large and filled with every book on every kind of animal and magical being you could think of. What Henry didn't know was that Theodore, Catherine, and even his mother were all hiding secrets from him—not just one, but two secrets that would turn his life upside down.

That night, he received a letter from Amara, saying how sorry she was that she couldn't come back with them, but she knew she had to stay where she was for now. Henry admired her heart; it was so pure and full of kindness, but he also feared that Amara might be a little naïve and very easy to manipulate, and Agnes could take advantage of that. He sent her a letter back, assuring her that he believed in her and would be waiting for her to come back home, to come back to him. Even though Henry wrote all of that in his letter to her, he felt differently. He still felt betrayed by Amara and jealous of Aiden. He didn't know what Aiden's intentions were with her, but he knew he didn't trust him.

They exchanged letters for days, and they both knew their feelings for each other were growing stronger with each passing day. They met a few times in person after Amara learned how to teleport between places.

Teleportation was a funny thing for witches. They could use it for short distances, but they never really figured out how to transport themselves between longer and unknown places.

Amara and Henry spent their time together getting to know each other better, walking hand in hand and stealing a kiss or two. They couldn't wait for the time they could finally be together, even though Henry could see Amara was starting to enjoy her time with Agnes and Aiden. He knew it was most likely because she could never really be herself in the castle.

One day, as they were walking through the woods, Henry asked Amara how Aiden was acting towards her and if he was nice to her. She stopped walking and let go of his hand.

"Yes, he's fine. He's just teaching me some spells and some history of magic. It is actually quite enjoyable," she smiled.

Henry didn't like the way she reacted when he asked her about him. He would have expected her to complain about him or show some form of dislike, but in fact, it was quite the opposite. She spoke about Aiden often, and it seemed they had grown closer.

Amara always said it was only as friends and that she liked him as her tutor. She insisted there was nothing more to it, but Henry knew that wasn't true. He could tell she had some kind of crush on him.

He decided not to ask her any more questions about Aiden. It infuriated him. Just thinking about the two of them together felt like someone was sticking a hot iron down his throat. Before either of them could say anything else, they stopped. They could hear heavy footsteps behind them, but they couldn't see anyone.

They frantically looked around, and instinctively, Henry stood in front of Amara to protect her. Then they saw it.

A large horse appeared before them. Upon closer inspection, they realised it wasn't a horse at all. It was a unicorn—not the one Amara had seen before and not the usual one Henry had read about in children's books. This one was enormous and black, with a white streak running through its tail. It had fiery orange eyes and sharp teeth, and it had a rider on its back. They couldn't tell if the rider was a man or a woman. The figure was dressed in black armour that covered their entire body, and their face was hidden by a black helmet. On their right side, they had a sword, and on their back rested a large black-silver shield.

"Who are you? What do you want?" asked Henry.

The rider said nothing and simply pointed at Amara.

Henry didn't have a sword or any other weapons on him. He turned to Amara and whispered, "Run."

He picked up a log lying nearby and stood firm, facing the unicorn and its master. He tried his best to fight, but he didn't stand a chance.

The unicorn reared up on its hind legs and kicked Henry so hard that he flew several metres away, hitting his head against a large rock. The rider then turned their attention to Amara, who was running through the woods, disoriented and unsure of where she was. Everything around her looked the same, and she feared she might be running straight towards danger.

In that moment, she wished she knew spells that could help her.

As she kept running, the unicorn suddenly appeared in front of her. The sight terrified Amara. She stumbled backwards, falling to the ground. The rider dismounted and walked towards her, grabbing her by her hair and dragging her towards a cliff. Amara kicked and screamed, but the rider was much stronger than she was.

When they reached the top of the cliff, Amara looked up and asked, "Why?"

The rider didn't respond. Instead, they drew a knife from their belt and stabbed Amara in the belly. She gasped, looked down, and a tear rolled down her cheek. The rider hesitated for a moment, as if weighing their options, but then they threw her off the cliff.

She was falling for what felt like an eternity, gazing up at the cliff above her before she hit the water below. The rider then leapt back onto their unicorn and flew away.

Amara was underwater, drowning. All she could

think about was that this was the end; no one could save her now.

She was drifting away when someone grabbed her hand and pulled her out of the water. She kept passing out and waking up, hearing a voice she recognised. It was Aiden, chanting.

He chanted louder and louder until Amara gasped deeply and opened her eyes. She sat up coughing up the water trapped in her lungs. She lifted her shirt, and saw that the wound had healed, but the area was still sore.

Aiden placed his hand on her back and asked, "What happened?"

Amara looked at him and, between coughs, replied, "I don't know. There was someone, and for some reason, they wanted to kill me."

"Who was it?" he asked.

"I don't know. I couldn't see their face, but they were riding a black unicorn."

Aiden suddenly looked troubled, his eyes wandering around.

"What is it? Who was that? And how did you know where I was?" she asked.

"I don't know who rides the black unicorn now, but whoever it is, they are dangerous."
He paused, stood up, and ran his hands through his hair. "I knew you were here because I had one of the ravens following you. I had to know you were safe at all times."

Amara wanted to be angry with Aiden for violating her privacy while she was with Henry, but he had saved her life, so she didn't say anything except, "Thank you."

"Why would they want to kill me?" she asked.

"I don't know, Amara, but we have to stay clear of the rider. Black unicorns are not the usual type you would know. They are foul, dangerous creatures. They choose their master, and whoever rides them is not a good or fair person."

Amara had never heard of them. Aiden explained that they were once white unicorns—pure beings— but their blood was corrupted by dark elves to serve in battles. From that point on, they became evil, existing in a state between death and life. There aren't many of them, but a few still remain. He hadn't seen one in years, and it wasn't good news when you did.

Whoever was riding this one must have found it somewhere and became its master. Only an evil person with a black heart would be accepted by a black unicorn.

Aiden picked her up and teleported them back to the cottage, where they told Agnes everything that had happened. Agnes didn't say much, but Aiden couldn't shake the feeling that she knew something she wasn't telling them.

CHAPTER 8

A Horrible Secret

After Mary recovered from her injuries, she made contact with Henry. She refused to come back to the castle, so Henry had to go to her.

They talked about everything that had happened, and she couldn't believe that Amara had chosen to stay behind. Mary wanted to know everything Henry had been up to while she was away, so he told her, but every other sentence ended up being about Amara—how much he missed her and how much he wanted to be with her again.

Mary couldn't hide her secrets any longer and decided to tell Henry the truth.

"Henry, we need to talk about Amara."

He looked at his mother, his eyebrows raised. "What do you mean?"

"You and she can't be together. I'm sorry."

"What are you talking about? Why can't we be together, Mum?"

Mary sat him down, massaging her forehead and breathing unevenly. She knew it was time to tell Henry the details about his father's death, why she couldn't return to the castle, and why she had asked Henry not to tell the King who his mother was. She asked him not to interrupt her until she had finished and to forgive her for not telling him earlier.

She began by explaining that seventeen years ago, when Henry was just one year old, his grandfather had passed away. His name was Leopold, and he was the King of the Gulrose Kingdom. When he died, one of his two sons was supposed to become the new ruler; however, this had to be decided by a duel as they were twins. Henry's father won and was set to be the next King, but on the morning of his coronation, he was killed. Mary feared that his brother had something to do with his death and that he would try to harm her and Henry—especially Henry, as he could claim the throne when he was older. In response, she ran to Theodore and asked him to protect them. He sent them to London and was sworn to secrecy.

"Your father's name was Peter, and your uncle—the one who ultimately became the King of Gulrose—is William. Amara's father is your father's brother. The two of you are cousins. That's why I can't go back and why William must not know who you are. He might still want to hurt you, especially now that you are old enough to lead and could challenge him for the throne."

"What? Why didn't you tell me this before? Before I fell for her?" asked Henry.

"I'm sorry I didn't tell you, but there's more."

"More? What else did you hide from me?"

Mary had tears streaming down her face. She felt horrible. She never wanted to lie to her son or hide the truth from him, but she had known she couldn't tell him until he was older and ready to handle it. She told him that now that he knew his true roots, he also needed to understand the curse running through his veins. She explained how all those in the royal family were shapeshifters, able to change from human to manticore. His father had been one, which meant that Henry was one too. So was William, and anyone else born into their bloodline.

"What's a manticore?" Henry asked.

"It's a beast. It has the body of a lion, bat-like wings, and a tail like a scorpion."

Henry's eyes widened. He didn't understand what this meant. Did this mean he could change into this animal? Why hadn't he done it before?

He started to breathe heavily; his head was spinning. He stood up and just ran. He could hear his mother shouting his name behind him, but he didn't care. He needed to be far away from her now. How could she not have told him this before?

He ran for what felt like hours until he couldn't run anymore. He fell to his knees and buried his head in his hands. Looking up at the sky, he punched the ground below him with his fists. He had never felt this heartbroken, angry, and scared all at once. All of this meant that he and Amara could never be together, and he had never felt more devastated. It also meant he was some kind of animal. The way his mother spoke about it, with fear in her voice and eyes, made it clear it couldn't be anything good. Would he know who he was when he changed? And how would he even change? He didn't know anything about this, but he knew the only person who could help him understand it all was Theodore. He had to learn everything about the creature he was supposed to have inside him. He had to talk to him, but first, he felt the need to do something else to clear his mind.

He stood up and started walking back to the castle. When he arrived, he grabbed his horse, Pearl, and the sword that had been given to him, then rode away. It was a cold afternoon with a strong wind.

Henry kept riding, trying to forget everything. Suddenly, his horse stopped and began backing up.

"Whoa, whoa, easy girl," said Henry, trying to calm Pearl down. But before he could do anything else, he saw it: a large black wolf. He froze for a second; he had never seen a wolf this big. It was almost as if it wasn't natural, like it couldn't be real.

The wolf was baring its teeth at Henry and Pearl. Heart racing, Henry jumped off his horse and drew his sword, hands shaking. He didn't know if he could protect himself and Pearl from it; he was only just starting to improve at his training, but he had to try. He held his sword the way the knights at the castle had taught him and began to step slowly and carefully forward.

But the wolf was fast. It lunged at Henry, knocking him to the ground. Its mouth was wide open, sharp teeth looming dangerously close to Henry's face. He thought this was the end. Closing his eyes, he made peace with his impending death. Just as the wolf pulled its head back, ready to attack, it suddenly stopped and turned, as if someone or something had interrupted it.

The ferocious wolf transformed from a predator into a frightened pup, backing away sheepishly and whimpering. Henry opened his eyes and followed the wolf's gaze. Standing nearby was a girl with long raven-black hair and ocean-blue eyes. She wore a flowing black dress and held out her hand before slowly lowering it back down. A witch. She stood there for a moment, looking at Henry, then turned and began to walk away.

Quickly, Henry stood up and called out, "Thank you!"

The girl turned around and winked at him.

He smiled and said, "I'm Henry, by the way."

"Eleanor," she replied with a small grin before continuing on her way.

Henry returned to Pearl, holding her reins and soothing her as she continued to fidget nervously. His gaze kept drifting back in the direction Eleanor had gone. Another witch.

There were no witches in Gulrose, at least none apart from Amara, Agnes, and Aiden. This could only mean one thing: they were on their way back. Amara was making progress, and soon she would be reunited with her family—she would be with him. Henry wasn't sure how he would break the news to her about what he had just learned, but he knew it couldn't wait.

He climbed back onto Pearl and rode swiftly to the castle. Once there, he went straight to Theodore's room, rapping firmly on the door.

"Come in," came a voice from inside.

Henry entered and shut the door behind him. He began pacing the room, his thoughts racing, until Theodore finally broke the silence.

"Stop at once and tell me what's on your mind."

Henry stopped and launched into everything his mother had just revealed. He assured Theodore that he wasn't angry—he understood that they both owed their survival to him. The conversation stretched on for hours as Theodore filled in more details about their family's history. By the end, Henry had one more revelation to share: the encounter with the witch who had saved his life in the woods.

"So, they're returning," Theodore mused. "Very well. We must be prepared."

"Prepared for what?" Henry asked, his curiosity heightened.

"For a battle, my boy. A battle," Theodore replied grimly.

Henry frowned. "What battle? Why would there be a battle?"

Theodore's answer was vague. He spoke of a dream he'd had about a witches' uprising and the need to be ready for their attack.

"Fine," Henry agreed. "I'll do whatever you need me to. But there's one more thing I need to talk to you about—and I need your help." His voice was steady, but serious.

"Anything, Henry. What is it?" Theodore asked, leaning forward.

Henry hesitated before speaking. "My mum told me that I'm also a… manti-something. I can't remember the exact name."

"Yes, yes. A manticore," Theodore said, removing his glasses and rubbing his forehead.

He took a deep breath, fully aware of the implications. Of course, Henry had to be one; his father was, and so was his uncle. Theodore walked over to his extensive collection of books and selected the volume he knew would provide answers. He opened it to a section dedicated entirely to manticores.

The legend of the manticores told of a curse born from betrayal and vengeance. Thousands of years ago, a witch named Talia fell deeply in love with King John, ruler of a kingdom that existed long before Gulrose. Believing he was her one true love; she was devastated to learn the harsh truth: he was using her magical powers to win his battles. His heart was never hers.

Furious and heartbroken, Talia sought vengeance. In her rage, she cursed the king and his entire bloodline, condemning them to transform into creatures of nightmare—half lion, half scorpion, with bat-like wings. Every blood relative of King John was doomed to bear this curse, transforming once a month during the New Moon. Initially, the king saw this transformation as a terrible fate, but he soon realised he could use it as a weapon.

Years passed, and King John found another witch who fell under his charm. Unaware of his true nature, she was tricked into helping him rewrite the curse. However, the ritual required a significant sacrifice—one of young magical blood—to succeed. In a twisted sense of poetic justice, the king decided that the offering should be Talia's own daughter, a child she had with another man after cursing him.

King John kidnapped Talia's daughter and sacrificed her on an altar during a dark ceremony. The spell worked. The manticores could now transform at will, making them even deadlier. But the cost was unimaginable. Talia, devastated by the loss of her child, could not bear her grief. She blamed herself for the tragedy and ultimately took her own life.

Talia was a direct ancestor of Agnes. That was why Agnes despised humans, particularly the royal family. The hatred ran in her blood—a legacy of vengeance passed down through generations.

"That's insane. Everyone in my family is mad, vengeful, and impulsive," Henry muttered, frustration bubbling to the surface.

He could see from Theodore's expression that he shared the sentiment. Sitting down, Henry bit his cheek, struggling to process the revelations. "So, how do I change into one?"

"You just do," Theodore replied, his tone steady. "The ability is within you."

Henry's mind raced with questions. "Wait—does that mean Amara is also a manticore, if her father is one?"

Theodore sighed. "Amara is a hybrid. She was born to be a manticore, but because of the potion Agnes made, she is also a witch. She is the first of her kind. Very powerful—and, when untrained or improperly trained, very dangerous."

This revelation crashed over Henry like a wave, leaving him gasping for breath. He couldn't bear the weight of it anymore. Standing abruptly, he muttered his apologies before leaving the room and heading to his own.

When he opened the door, he was taken aback. Amara sat in one of his chairs, and when she caught sight of him, her smile faded.

"Is everything all right?" she asked.

Henry shut the door behind him, his heart racing as he approached her. He opened his mouth to speak but hesitated, unsure how to explain everything he had learned.

After a moment, he took a deep breath, forcing himself to meet her gaze.

"Amara, there's so much I need to tell you... about me, about us."

And he did. He told her everything. They held hands, their hearts breaking. They knew they couldn't be together, but they also knew that was all they wanted.

"I'm a... a hybrid?"

"Yes. You're half-manticore and half-witch. The first of your kind," he replied.

Amara couldn't believe it. Surely Agnes knew. Why hadn't she told her?

They sat in silence for a while until Amara suddenly stood up, wiped her tears away, said goodbye, and disappeared into thin air, leaving Henry teary and trembling.

She teleported to the woods near Agnes's house and wandered aimlessly. She couldn't believe it. She had thought Henry was the man she was meant to be with, but now she wondered if that feeling was because they were related. Perhaps that was why they had shared such a special connection. Or was it because they were shapeshifters, both manticores?

She broke down, crying as these thoughts overwhelmed her, and sat beneath a tall birch tree.

"Amara?" came a voice from behind her. She recognised it instantly—it was Aiden. He walked over slowly, knelt down, and placed his hands gently on her knees. He asked what had happened and whether someone had hurt her. The rage on his face at the thought of her being harmed was unmistakable.

Amara told him everything. He sighed deeply, then sat down beside her and wrapped his arms around her in a tight hug. For the first time, Amara truly felt like Aiden was her friend, like she was safe with him.

"Did you know?" she asked, wiping away her tears.

"Yes," he admitted.

"All of it? About whom Henry really is and what we are?"

"Yes. And I'm sorry. I wasn't allowed to tell you; my mother forbade it."

Amara couldn't believe it. Why was Agnes keeping this from her?

They stayed under the tree all night, talking. As the sun began to rise, they made their way back to the house. More than ever, Amara was determined to practise magic. She remembered how powerful she felt whenever she used spells, and she longed for that feeling again.

She wanted to feel in control. Most importantly, she wanted to learn how to shapeshift.

At first, she and Aiden practised simple spells, but she quickly grew frustrated with the trivial incantations that offered no real protection for her or the people she cared about. She wanted to do more.

"What's that?" she asked, pointing to a black book behind Aiden.

"Oh, this? That's something I was studying earlier, but I don't want you getting involved with it," Aiden said.

"Why not?" Amara pressed.

"It's the dark spellbook. It's very powerful—and dangerous."

That was exactly what Amara needed. Learning the truth about herself had left her heartbroken; it ignited a craving for danger within her.

Amara asked Aiden to teach her something from the book. He hesitated. She was pure, and he didn't want to tarnish her. Yet, he also recognised her strength and the immense power his mother had infused into the potion all those years ago. Amara could become the most powerful witch the world had ever seen. With her on their side, they would be unstoppable.

Reluctantly, Aiden opened the book and found a spell he deemed suitable.

"Alright. I think you should try this one."

"What does it do?" she asked.

"This spell closes someone's airways—human or animal—so they can't breathe. It's incredibly useful in a fight."

"I don't want to do that. That's evil," Amara said firmly.

"I thought you wanted to feel the power. This will give it to you, and you can stop after a few seconds—no harm done. Come on, try it on me."

Amara sighed, then picked up the book. She read the spell silently a few times until she felt confident enough to begin.

"Satta i halsen, satta i halsen,"

She raised her hand, directing it towards Aiden, and repeated the spell over and over. Suddenly, Aiden began to choke, clutching his throat. Yet, he didn't appear frightened; instead, he looked proud.

Amara's face lit up. She felt it—the power coursing through her veins—and she liked it. She stopped the spell, and Aiden fell to his knees.

He looked up at her and smiled. For the first time, Aiden didn't see Amara as a pawn to reclaim their power but as a woman—a sensual woman standing above him, radiating strength. He felt an unexpected attraction to her.

Rising to his feet, he stepped closer, gently took her chin in his hand, and looked intensely into her eyes.

"You… are extraordinary, Amara. Powerful, beautiful, intriguing."

Her cheeks flushed crimson. He stepped closer, placing a hand on her waist, his gaze locked with hers as his lips inched nearer. She stood frozen, unmoving. He leaned closer still, their lips barely touching, then they kissed. Their bodies pressed together; their breaths were heavy. Aiden tangled his fingers in her hair, pulling her closer.

When they finally parted, they stared into each other's eyes, their emotions a confusing swirl. Neither of them understood what this meant. They had never felt an attraction to each other before, but now something new and undeniable lingered between them.

Aiden turned away and walked back into the house. Amara remained rooted to the spot, stunned. She had never experienced anything like this before. Her first and only kiss had been with Henry—a sweet, intimate exchange between two people with genuine feelings for each other. But this kiss was something else entirely.

It was rough and seductive, yet sweet and gentle all at once. Aiden had never approached her like this before. She raised her hand to her lips, brushing them with her middle and index fingers, and let out a soft, incredulous chuckle.

But then another emotion took hold—betrayal.

She began pacing back and forth slowly. She felt as though she had betrayed Henry. They couldn't be together, but she still cared deeply for him. Her feelings for Aiden were nothing like that. It wasn't love; it wasn't affection. It was attraction. Lust.

Aiden was strong, commanding, and unafraid to take what he wanted. He made her feel the power that coursed through her veins, and she liked it.

CHAPTER 9

The Girl in the Woods

Henry lay on his bed, thinking about Amara. He couldn't believe she had left the day before after learning the truth.

It wasn't as though they were siblings. Yes, they were cousins, but they hadn't grown up together; they barely knew each other. He couldn't help himself—he still wanted her. Learning the truth hadn't changed his feelings. He knew it wasn't right, but he didn't care as much as he probably should. He had never felt for anyone the way he felt for her. She was the first girl he had ever liked.

When he woke up that morning, the only thing on his mind was getting dressed and training. He grabbed his sword, Pearl, and rode into the woods. There, he began practising with his sword, lunging and slicing through the air. He had found his calling.

Being alone in the woods, honing his skills, cleared his mind and brought him peace.

He had always possessed a strange gift—the ability to hear and see things others couldn't. He had never understood why and had simply accepted it. Now, of course, he knew the reason. This newfound knowledge made him more confident in his abilities: to train, to avoid danger, and to survive. Suddenly he paused, sensing something—or someone—approaching. Then he saw her. It was Eleanor.

"Well, well, well. You, again. In our woods," she said, striding closer to him.

"I'm sorry, I didn't know these were your woods. Actually, I don't think anyone knows that." He replied.

"You are very, very brave to speak like this to a witch."

"No, not brave. Just a bit dense sometimes."

Eleanor found herself intrigued by him. Of course, he was tall and handsome, but it wasn't just that. He had spirit, courage, and a sharp wit. She walked over to Pearl and began scratching her neck, just behind her ear. Henry leaned on his sword, watching her closely.

Eleanor was a strikingly beautiful girl. She reminded him a little of Amara—not just because of the magic, but because they looked similar, apart from their hair and eyes.

"What's on your mind?" she asked, still scratching Pearl.

"What are you doing here? Did you come to Gulrose alone? Are you here to stay?" he asked.

Eleanor laughed and sat down on the grass, gesturing for Henry to sit next to her.

When he did, she explained that she had come with her father. They had heard about Amara and the chance to rebuild their coven. Eleanor was from here. They were a big family of five: her, her mother, her father, and her twin brothers. When the witches were attacked, her mother and brothers had died. It was only she and her father who had survived. He had taken her and ran. Now they were back, hoping to stay.

Henry asked if she had met Amara yet and wondered if they had gotten along, but she told him they hadn't met yet. For now, all the witches were staying in the forest, and they were all going to meet Amara, Agnes, and Aiden the next day.

They talked some more. Henry told her about London and about his father.

She was intrigued by London and kept asking different questions.

"Do you have fairies? How do you travel between places? Have you ever seen a wolf? How about a centaur?"

Henry chuckled and happily answered each of her questions. She couldn't believe there was a place without witches. They had a good time together and talked for hours before Eleanor said she needed to go; otherwise, her father would be worried.

They said their goodbyes, and she left. He watched her as she walked away, a warmth filling his cheeks. He cracked his knuckles, shook his head, and picked up his sword again. He practised for another hour before heading back to the castle. On his way, he couldn't help but chuckle to himself. Eleanor had made him realise that maybe there was more out there than Amara. They couldn't be together anyway, so what was the harm in meeting and getting to know someone new?

The next day, as Eleanor had said, all the witches who had once had to run from their homes arrived at Agnes's cottage. There were around fifty of them.

They began to rebuild their roots, starting with a — a mansion so large that every witch and sorcerer who wished to join their coven could call it home. It was black, with a grey roof and a brown door. Inside, they built a great library filled with grimoires from different magical families of the past. This was going to be their kingdom. Amara thought it was beautiful how everyone came together to start rebuilding their lives.

What she didn't know was that Agnes's intentions weren't as pure as she made her believe. Yes, she wanted to gather all of her kind and gain power to live in peace, but she also wanted revenge—revenge on all those who had slain her friends and family twenty years ago, and also on the kin of those who had caused her descendant's death. She wanted a war that she, Aiden, and Amara would lead. Agnes believed that with enough persuasion and a show of power, she would join them.

Amara stood outside the Black Mansion when she saw Aiden. She walked up to him and asked him to go into the forest with her so they could talk.

When they arrived, she said, "Tell me how to change."

"What? What do you mean?"

"You know what I mean. Tell me how to change into a manticore."

Aiden wasn't sure if he should tell her how to change. His mother wouldn't be pleased. She just wanted Amara to do spells; she didn't want her to become one of them, but he couldn't resist her. He had the urge to do anything she asked of him.

He looked around to make sure no one was watching them, then came closer to her and whispered in her ear, "It's in you; you just have to find that place. Dig deep, and you will be able to change. It's in your blood, but I warn you, it will be painful—very painful."

Amara swallowed hard and nodded. They walked deeper into the forest so no one would hear her screams.

When they were far enough, she closed her eyes, took a deep breath, and tried to find the place inside her where the manticore was hidden. They stood there for a while, but nothing was happening. She squinted her eyes as she tried harder, but it didn't work. She kept failing.

She grew angry and screamed. She was angry that she couldn't change and frustrated with Aiden for not helping her enough.

"Don't think too hard about this, Amara. Just think of a moment that made you feel powerful. Find a memory that filled you with strength."

Amara thought about this for a second, and the only time she truly felt powerful was when she practised a choking spell from the dark spellbook on Aiden. She recalled how his face changed colours when she held his life in her palm. She closed her eyes again, took a deep breath, and focused on that moment. She envisioned her veins tingling as the power filled her body and the look of pride on Aiden's face.

Then she felt a strange sensation. She stretched her neck and wore a little frown. Aiden was watching her, sensing that something was happening. He took a few steps back.

Suddenly, Amara put her hand on her stomach and leaned forward. She shrieked and painfully walked over to a tree to lean on. Then she lifted her head, exposing her eyes to Aiden. They were no longer green; now they were dark orange. He took a few more steps back, as if he knew what was coming, as if he had seen this before.

Her teeth changed from perfect shapes to long canines with sharp tips and edges. She was changing. She fell to her knees, and her back began to form a different shape.

Claws started to grow on her hands, which were changing into paws. The whole transformation took about half an hour, but for Amara, it felt like much longer than that. It was the most painful thing she had ever gone through. She screamed, cried, and pleaded for it to stop. Aiden had to close his eyes frequently and turn away; he couldn't watch her in pain.

When she was fully transformed, he just stood there and kept looking at her. He loved the view. So powerful, a true queen. Amara kept looking at him for a while, then she ran away. She ran fast, feeling the wind in her mane. The ground under her paws felt strange. She ran faster and faster, enjoying every second of this new life she had discovered. Aiden knew she wouldn't come back for hours, but he also knew she would need some clothes when she returned to her human form.

He went back inside the mansion to grab some and then returned to the spot where Amara had changed. He waited for a few hours, reading through the dark grimoire.

Suddenly, he heard a noise, and when he turned, he saw her. Amara had returned. She stood next to him for a few seconds before transforming back into her human form. Aiden turned away so she could get dressed.

"So, how was it?" he asked.

"I've never felt anything like this. I felt so free. So strong," she said, breathing heavily.

"You can't tell Mother you transformed. She won't like it."

"Why not? Don't you understand? As a hybrid, no one will ever dare cross witches again with me by your side," said Amara.

Aiden thought about this and realised she was right. She already had so much power as a witch, but manticores were also very powerful. They were fast, strong, and cunning. He knew that the whole of the royal family were manticores, and even though they had many witches on their side, he wasn't sure if magic would be enough once they transformed.

They went back to speak with Agnes and tell her.

Agnes wasn't happy about this. She didn't want Amara to be spoiled. Right now, she thought of her as pure with her magic, but manticores were unnatural; they were beasts, so she forbade Amara from ever changing again.

"We will win with our magic if there is a battle. You don't have to change into one of these beasts," said Agnes.

Amara didn't like this. This was who she was supposed to be before Agnes made her a witch. She hoped there would be no battle and that she would be able to go home, but she didn't really know if she wanted to. It seemed to her that no matter where she was, she couldn't be herself. With Agnes, she couldn't be a manticore, and in a castle, she couldn't be a witch. Where was her place in the world then? Where could she be free?

She didn't know that, while all of this was on her mind, the King was holding a council meeting with the leaders of the surrounding kingdoms. He was aware of the incoming witches and what they were capable of.

They had to come up with a plan of attack. They couldn't wait for them to strike first. Armies from all the kingdoms, united, were once again plotting a war against the witches. After a very heated debate, it was decided that all the armies would gather and attack in two days' time.

After the meeting, the King went to see Catherine. He wanted to talk to her about the plan to get Amara out of there before the battle.

"Why does there have to be a war?" Catherine asked.

"Why does there have to be a war? Because if we don't strike, they will do it when we least expect it, when we are vulnerable, and they will take the kingdom for themselves. They will kill us all if we give them the chance."

"Maybe they only want to unite and be at peace with humans," she said.

William walked slowly over to Catherine and chuckled. He put his hand over his mouth and looked up at the ceiling, shaking his head. He closed his eyes, and when he opened them again, Catherine could see the rage within him. It was all over his face.

"You're so daft, Catherine. You didn't grow up with the witches like I did." He pointed at his chest. "All they know and want is power, and if we don't play by their rules, they will ruin us and our families. My father did the right thing all those years ago when he rid us of all of them."

Catherine had no words. Was he right? Was this the only option they had?

The only thing she could think about was Amara. If war was coming, she needed to get her daughter out of there.

After the meeting with the King, Catherine went to see Henry. She rushed to his room and knocked on his door. She didn't wait for him to invite her in; she opened the door and shut it firmly and quickly behind her. Henry was sitting on his bed, reading a history book. When he saw her, he looked up and closed his book.

"What's happened? Are you okay?"

Catherine sat down next to him and told him what had been discussed during the council meeting. She told him they had to get Amara out now; otherwise, she would get caught up in the middle of this war, and Catherine feared it would cost Amara her life.

"I know the truth now," said Henry.

"What truth?"

"My mother told me everything about me, Amara, and the manticores."

Catherine nodded. She knew Mary would have to tell him at some point. He and Amara were growing closer to each other every day. They had to know they were cousins, and with the war coming, it was good that he knew about the curse. Henry stood up and walked over to his window, running his hand through his hair. Then he turned and looked at Catherine.

"Did he do it? Did William kill my father?"

"I don't know, Henry. I don't think he did. I don't think he would be able to hurt his own brother. He can be cruel and vengeful, but he did love your father."

"Then who did? And why?"

Catherine sat there and watched Henry, who drew his lips in tightly. He had never got to meet his father. She wanted to comfort him, but there was a sudden knock on his door.

"Come in," said Henry to whoever was on the other side of the door.

The door opened, and in walked Theodore. He asked if he could speak to Henry alone for a minute. Catherine touched Henry's hand lightly, smiled, and left the room.

When they were alone, Theodore opened his satchel and took out several leather notebooks. "These were your father's. He loved writing in his diaries. I found them in his chambers a day after he was murdered, and I know now that you know the truth about yourself; he would want you to have them."

"Oh, thank you."

Theodore smiled, stood up, and left the room so Henry could be alone. He looked at the notebooks, took a deep breath, and opened the first one. It was dated a few years before Henry was born. Henry started to read the first page.

July 1977

"Today was a good day. I have met the love of my life. Her name is Mary. She is a lady from the Dodblomma Kingdom. She arrived here with the

princess I was supposed to marry, but how could I, when I saw this beauty today? No one even compares to her and her kind heart. I know we will be together, and she will make me the happiest man alive."

Henry smiled. It was strange but nice to read his father's thoughts about his mother. Now more than ever, he wished his father were still alive and that he could see his parents happy together.

He skipped a few pages and found an interesting one.

December 1979

"Today was a cold night. I shapeshifted. I love the feeling when I can run free. When I was younger and our father told me and William what we were, I hated it, but now I love it. There is no better feeling than running free in the wild and feeling that power. That strength. I can't wait to run with my children one day."

Henry knew he would read them all in detail at some point, but right now he wanted to know if his father mentioned anything that might lead Henry to his murderer.

The notebooks were numbered by year, starting with 1973. He picked up a notebook with the year 1983, the year his father was murdered, when Henry was 1 year old.

August 1983

"I have a strange feeling. I feel like I am being followed by someone or something. Shapeshifting was a way to clear my head, but now whenever I change, I feel something. I don't know who or what it is, but I know I might be in danger. I think someone wants to hurt me, but I don't know why."

Henry was shocked. So, his father knew someone was after him? He kept going through the pages, hoping to find more. He hadn't come here to avenge his father, but as he read, he knew he wanted to find that person and make them pay. Another knock on his door startled him. It was Catherine again.

"I just came back to make sure you're alright before I go to bed," she said.

"I think I am, thank you. I just keep learning stuff I didn't know about myself and my family every day. It's like I am getting hit all the time."

"I know, and I know it's hard, but we have to think of a way to get Amara out of there. We have to save her. I want my daughter here, with me."

"I know, but I'm not sure if it isn't too late."

"What do you mean by that?" asked Catherine.

Henry looked at her and bit his cheek. "I think she likes Aiden, and I think she likes the power. There is something different about her. Something has changed."

They had a long conversation, trying to figure out how best to approach Amara and convince her to come back home as soon as possible, where she belonged.

When Catherine left to go to bed, Amara appeared in Henry's bedroom shortly after. He was happy to see her; he missed her, but her face showed she felt differently.

"We need to talk," she said.

"Yes, we do. Please sit down."

Amara walked over to a chair and took a seat. She looked down at her hands, then back at Henry, frowning. "I have to stop coming here for a while. I need to concentrate on my training if I want to help them, and I can't do that if I keep disappearing to meet you all the time."

She paused for a moment. "I also need to stop coming here so I can stop feeling the way I do about you."

Henry's heart broke all over again. He felt like he couldn't take this anymore. He stood up and walked over to Amara. He knelt before her, grabbed her face, looked deep into her eyes, and kissed her. It was different from when she kissed Aiden; this kiss was short and sweet, innocent.

When they stopped, Henry looked at her and said, "I understand, but you have to stay here. You can't go back. There will be a war between humans and witches, and you can't be in the middle of that. It will be dangerous, and blood will be spilled. Please come back here, where you are safe, where I can protect you."

Amara's face changed; she was confused. "What war? What are you talking about?"

"Your father decided it today during a council meeting. They will attack the witches to drive them out of the Gulrose again, just like they did all those years ago," he said.

"No, they can't do that! They just can't!" Amara panicked; she didn't want to choose a side, and she didn't want humans to start this war.

"I have to go. I have to warn them."

Before Henry could stop her, she disappeared, but he couldn't even worry anymore. He was so tired after the day he had that he fell asleep.

Amara teleported straight to the Black Mansion. She ran inside and told Agnes everything she had learned that evening. She was distraught; she didn't want to fight against her family, but she had to do what was right. She had to protect them from her father's madness. This played well into Agnes' plan. She had always wanted a war between witches and humans, but now it would look like the King was the one waging the war, and the witches would only fight to protect themselves. It was perfect.

"Then we must be prepared for war," she said, "and you must choose a side."

Amara didn't want to choose. This was between her family and her witch family, and her father was the one who started this, not the witches. So, even though she didn't want to, she had to do what she thought was right.

"I will fight with you if it comes to it," she said.

Agnes was pleased, and so was Aiden. They had to prepare; there was a lot of work to be done. They had to gather more witches, so they sent out word about the impending war and the plan for Gulrose to become a witch land once again after they won the fight against humans.

Over a hundred witches gathered and prepared for what was coming, while Amara and Aiden were in the woods practising. Aiden taught her how to set something on fire, how to stop someone from moving, and other spells useful for the upcoming fight.

"I want you to teach me one more spell," she said.

"No problem, what is it?" he asked.

"I want you to teach me a protection spell. The big one."

And so, Aiden did. Amara learned how to protect those she loved. She knew the war was imminent, and she would have to face her father and the soldiers from other kingdoms. She was hoping Henry wouldn't get involved, but she had to make sure she could protect him too if it came to that.

CHAPTER 10

Diaries From The Dead

When Henry woke up in the morning, he knew that he had to try to shapeshift that day.

It would be an advantage for him during the battle; it was who he was and who his father had been. So, he went to see his mother, thinking she could help him. When he arrived, she hugged him and sobbed. This was the longest she had ever been apart from her son, and she wasn't coping well without him. She first apologised for not telling him the whole truth earlier; she had been scared of how he would react.

Henry understood. It didn't make it easier, but he understood. He told his mother that Catherine had spoken to William. He now knew who Henry and Mary really were, and he told her they were both welcome in the castle.

She hesitated. She still didn't completely believe that William had nothing to do with Peter's murder, but in the end, she agreed. She wanted to be with her son, especially with the war looming. Henry helped her pack her things, she thanked her friend for taking care of her, said her goodbyes, and then headed back to the castle.

While they were walking, Henry asked her if she knew how his father had transformed into a manticore.

Mary didn't like this question. She had never liked Peter's ability to change. To her, it felt unnatural, an abomination. She didn't want her son to undergo that transformation or endure the associated pain, and she expressed all of this to Henry.

Keeping his head down, Henry avoided making eye contact with his mother. This was who he was, and his mother hated it. Now he understood how Amara must have felt all those years when her father rejected who she was and tried to make her into someone else.

He recognised that his ability was not entirely normal, and he was still trying to wrap his head around it himself, but this was who his father had been, and she had loved him—she had married him. How could she be so opposed to it?

Henry thought he might be able to find more details in his father's diaries. For now, he didn't tell his mother that he had them; he needed them, and she would want to read them. He couldn't give them up now—not until he had read everything.

They continued walking for a while before they reached the castle. As they entered, Mary appeared as white as a ghost. She was terrified.

They stood in the great hall for a little while when suddenly they heard footsteps. Mary took a few steps back. Henry noticed this, stepped back as well, and took her hand.

"Mary, it's good to have you back here. We have your chambers ready for you. You are safe and welcome here," said William as he appeared from around the corner, with Catherine by his side.

"Thank you, Your Majesty. It is good to be back," she replied, bowing slightly.

William could tell that she only called him that out of royal protocol. He knew she still believed he had something to do with his brother's murder.

The staff arrived, picked up her luggage, and escorted her to her room.

Catherine and William left the hall and went into the library, hoping to find more information on how to face the witches and retrieve their daughter.

In the meantime, Henry returned to his room to read more of Peter's diaries. He picked up the first diary his father had ever written, which he had started when he was only thirteen years old. Henry opened the first page and began to read.

April 1973

"Father told me and William what we are today. I have heard of manticores before, but I always thought they were folklore. I never imagined I could be one. I still don't know the full story of how this curse happened, but maybe I will one day.

I have to admit, I am a bit scared. Does it hurt? How long can I stay like that? What if I can't change back? William seems much more excited about this than me. He already talked about the power we will have and how scared everyone will be.

I don't know why, but I have a gut feeling this will not bring anything good to us."

So, Henry's father had learned about the curse when he was thirteen. Henry wondered if he could find an entry about Peter's first change. He flipped through a few more pages until he found it.

September 15th, 1973

"Father promised me and William today that he will teach us how to change. He said it is important for young men to know how to run free and how to welcome the manticore within them. I am quite excited. I know it will probably be painful, but both William and I are strong. I know we can handle this. Father said we have to think of a moment where we felt the most powerful. He wants to go deeper into the woods so no one would hear us scream. Apparently, the first change is extremely painful. He said every bone in your body breaks to be able to regenerate itself and make you into a manticore.

That doesn't sound very appealing, does it? Oh well, I have no choice, do I? It's not like I could refuse this legacy—my father wouldn't allow me."

September 16th, 1973

"Yesterday was the worst and the best day of my life. I have changed. It was painful. My whole body rebuilt itself. I thought the pain would never stop, but then, as I was in my full form, different feelings rushed over my body—joy, strength, confidence. I was something new, something I didn't yet understand. I was fast and large. I could hear and see what I couldn't before. I know everyone says this is a curse, and yes, it's not very pleasant to change; it hurts, but after? You forget all about the pain and the aches. You only think about everything you could do in your other form. The armies you could lead, the enemies you could destroy.

I struggled to change at first, but William did not. He was always ahead of me with everything. Father told us the key to changing successfully is to have a strong memory. A memory where you felt the most powerful. You have to let it fuel your body and feel it in your veins. Then you will change.

I don't know what memory William chose. At first, I couldn't think of anything powerful enough, but then I remembered. A few years ago, William and I were riding in the woods. It was the first time we were allowed to go into the forest alone, and it was also the first time we had ever seen it—a wolf. Not the usual type you would see, the normal-sized, grey wolf. This was nothing like that. It was more like a bear. It was at least five times larger than a normal wolf and it was black with yellow eyes. It just stood there, growling. We stood frozen for a while, but then I took a few steps towards it and just stared it right in the eyes, not moving. I stood my ground, and after a while, the wolf went away. I have never felt more powerful. I used this memory.

I never understood why the wolf backed off. Maybe he could feel the animal inside of me?

Are manticores more dangerous than wolves? I might ask Theodore. He knows everything."

Henry now knew what he must do to change, but he wasn't sure if he even had a memory that made him feel truly powerful. Theodore had already been serving the kingdom when his father was young, and

Henry thought it would be wise to speak with him about this.

What if he didn't have a memory like that? Did it mean he would not be able to change—perhaps ever?

He opened another diary and read through the first page.

April 12th, 1975

"It was our birthday today. We had a great celebration and then I and William went into the forest. We ran together as brothers, feeling the freedom under our paws.

The pain is bearable now. It gets better with time. William and I ran through the woods when we encountered a girl. She was probably a few years younger than us, just sitting on the ground, playing. We didn't want to scare her—well, at least I didn't.

I started to back off when she noticed us, but William didn't. He slowly started coming closer and closer to her. You could see the fear in her face; she sat frozen, not moving. William was inches from her face when he let out the loudest roar I have ever heard. The girl burst into tears, shaking. William looked at her and backed off, and then we ran back to the other part of the forest and changed back into our human form.

While getting dressed, I confronted William. I asked why he had done that. He just laughed and said it was a bit of fun. I didn't push it, but that day I saw a part of my brother I didn't know, and I didn't like. Making a little innocent girl think she's about to be killed by a beast, eaten alive. Who would do that?"

Henry closed the diaries and made his way to see Theodore. With the battle set for the next day, he needed to know how to change. He knocked on his door, then stepped inside.

"Hello, Henry. How can I help you, my boy?" asked Theodore.

"I went through some of my dad's diaries. Thank you for giving them to me. I feel so much closer to him now."

"It was my pleasure. I knew he would want you to have them. For you to get to know him, at least in this way."

"Theodore, you knew my father when he first learned about being a manticore?"

Theodore took a deep breath, smiled, and replied, "Oh yes, yes, I did. I was only young myself—26 years old. I'd just been assigned as a tutor to your grandfather, and later to your father and uncle. I could tell from early on that your father was quite different from his brother."

"What do you mean, different?"

"Your father was very compassionate, Henry. He cared deeply about people's feelings, and he felt their sorrows as if they were his own. Your uncle, on the other hand, relished feeling powerful and rarely concerned himself with the emotions of others."

Henry felt proud of being his father's son. He was always very compassionate himself, and he liked the idea of his father being kind. On the other hand, he felt bad for Amara. If her father was still like this, she probably hadn't had the best childhood without her mother.

He asked Theodore about his father's struggles with shapeshifting. Theodore told him it had taken his father a while, and that William had succeeded first, probably because his father didn't think of things like power in the same way.

"I don't think I have a powerful memory like that," said Henry.

"When the time comes, you will find it, and it will lead you to your true self."

"The battle is tomorrow, Theodore. I don't have time to wait—I need to be able to change."

"Dig deep, Henry. It doesn't have to be only a memory of physical power. It can be a moment when you felt most powerful within yourself. That's what gives you power—courage, compassion, kindness."

Henry thanked Theodore and left. He didn't see himself as the most heroic person. He loved books and stories; he loved nature, and though he was training to be a knight, he didn't think of himself as brave.

He returned to his room and read more of his father's diaries. After a few hours, he ventured into the forest. He tried his hardest, but nothing was happening.

He decided to explore the surroundings a bit before going back to the castle. In the distance, he saw lights, and as he got closer, he witnessed the most beautiful scene: tiny lights flickering through the air. Fireflies?

He came closer and realised it wasn't fireflies—it was tiny people. He squinted and murmured, "It can't be... Fairies?"

Yes, he was sure of it. They were fairies, flitting from flower to flower, from tree to tree. He sat down and simply watched. In that moment, all his troubles, doubts, and fears disappeared.

One of the fairies noticed Henry and flew over to him, stopping directly in front of him and staring. Henry could tell it was a female fairy. She looked deeply into his eyes and tilted her head, as if she were thinking hard. Then she bounced, her eyes widening as if she had suddenly recognised him. She flew over to the other fairies and began whispering. Henry watched, confused. He stood up and moved closer to them, but as he did, they all scattered and flew away. He just stood there, marvelling at how strange the encounter had been.

He approached one of the flowers nearby. It emitted a soft, bright light, enchanting him. He felt compelled to pick one. He knelt down, but before he could reach it, he changed his mind. Something inside him told him to leave the flower alone, and so he did. He stood, looked around him, and, seeing no sign of the fairies, turned back towards the castle. The whole way back, he could only think about why he hadn't picked the flower. What was the voice inside his head that had told him not to, and why?

CHAPTER 11

Spilled Blood

The morning of the battle had arrived. Everyone was preparing for the attack, donning armour, sharpening swords.

Henry had volunteered to be part of his uncle's army, knowing he needed to be in the thick of the fight, close enough to protect Amara—if he could.

As he was strapping on his armour, gathering his courage, Amara appeared silently behind him. Henry froze, sensing her presence, and turned to face her. For a moment, he just looked, speechless. She didn't look like the fragile, sweet girl he'd met on that train in London. Now, a powerful woman stood before him. She wore a long-sleeved black dress, with a black cloak draped over her shoulders. Half of her hair was braided, while the rest cascaded freely down her back. At her hip, a sword gleamed on one side, and a small knife was strapped to the other. Her entire stance exuded readiness for battle.

"Why are you here?" Henry asked, his voice cold, restrained.

"I had to come and see you before... well, you know," she replied softly.

"I know. I wish we didn't have to be on different sides. We should fight together, not against each other. How could you choose them over your own family?" Henry snapped, his voice edged with hurt and frustration.

"It's not about choosing a side, Henry. It's about doing what is right. I didn't choose anyone," Amara said sharply. "It's my father who is waging this war—not the witches."

Both were visibly frustrated, and they no longer seemed to understand one another. The closeness they once shared seemed to be slipping away.

Amara sighed, then stepped forward and embraced Henry, pressing a gentle kiss to his cheek. In her heart, she knew that if they both survived this battle, things would never be the same between them. She took a last, lingering look at him before turning and vanishing into thin air, leaving Henry standing alone.

Meanwhile, William sought out Theodore to discuss strategies for the battle. He needed a way to make the witches more vulnerable in the fight. Luckily for him, Theodore already had a plan. Though he was conflicted about turning against his own kind, he understood the stakes. If he did nothing, all humans might fall.

He offered his services to the King, telling him he would be there during the fight and would use the spell he had used on Agnes to freeze her on as many of them as he could, giving humans a fighting chance. It would at least immobilise them for a little while. William knew it wasn't enough, but he also knew it was better than nothing, and it would give them a chance to slay them while they couldn't move.

Before the battle, Amara was in Agnes's room, searching through her belongings. She was trying to find the real pendant, feeling an uneasy suspicion about Agnes over the last few days, especially since Agnes had forbidden her from shapeshifting. Amara wanted to believe in Agnes's goodness, but a little voice inside urged her to be cautious, to have a backup plan just in case. Finding the pendant, however, proved harder than she expected; it was nowhere to be found. As she left the room, she ran into Aiden. After a brief exchange, she said, "You know what I've been thinking about?"

"How good I look?" Aiden smirked.

Amara smiled, shook her head, and replied, "No, not quite. I was thinking about the pendant. It was so beautiful I wanted to see it again—maybe study it a little. I bet it has more power than we were told."

"I don't know where it is," Aiden replied. "My mother's got it hidden somewhere."

"Ah, speaking of which, where is your mother?"

"Well, we didn't have the numbers we wanted, so she went to an old friend to see if they would join us."

"An old friend? What friend?" Amara raised an eyebrow.

"You'll see soon enough. She should be here any moment—hopefully with them."

Amara didn't know what he was talking about. She thought it would only be witches fighting, but she had to admit their numbers were much smaller than her father's army.

Suddenly, they heard a loud chime; she knew it was time. She went outside to meet the rest of the coven, and together they ventured through the woods. She saw Agnes already standing in front, leading them all.

Around five hundred soldiers were marching through the forest, much closer to the witches than they knew. They met in the middle of a field next to the woods. William marched first, with his army standing firmly behind him. Agnes walked up to meet him in the middle.

"There is still time to avoid this bloodbath, Agnes. Tell all the witches to leave Gulrose, return my daughter to me, and this war does not have to happen," said William.

Agnes chuckled. "Of course, it has to happen. You have sat on that throne for far too long after your father murdered innocent witches and their children for his own gain of power. We are taking our kingdom back, and you will bow to me. And your daughter? She will be the most powerful witch there ever was, and she will despise you after today. Don't say I didn't warn you."

Agnes looked up at the sky, lifted her hands, and closed her eyes. A clear blue sky suddenly changed; it started to rain, and the sky filled with dark clouds. William looked up, glanced back at Agnes, and rode his horse to his guards. They all stood strong, prepared for their King to call on them to fight. Before he could do anything, the ground started to shake.

Something big was coming. At first, they could only hear loud neighs, then they saw it: centaurs. More than fifty of them marched through the forest to aid Agnes, their bows and swords at the ready, travelling with such speed that the trees seemed to sway with them.

William couldn't believe it; he had never seen a centaur before, and he didn't think they were real. Suddenly, he felt a fear he hadn't felt before, but deep inside he knew he couldn't back down now; they had to attack and destroy them all.

He gave the signal. Sixty archers aimed their bows and shot their arrows, but it was in vain. Amara used a protection spell Aiden had taught her for all the witches on the field beside her, so no one was hurt. The arrows bounced off nothingness in front of them. The King looked at his daughter with anger and disgust on his face. She looked back, standing strong, not backing down.

Next to him, she saw Henry—her kind and sweet Henry. She kept looking at him, her eyes filling with tears.

He looked at her with despair, as if he were begging her to leave. They could feel each other, even standing far apart, but there was no coming back now. They had both chosen their sides, and they knew they would have to face each other.

William drew his sword and shouted for his soldiers to move forward. At the same time, the witches did the same. Both sides began to pick up the pace, with centaurs running in front of the witches. They were, of course, much faster, so they reached the army before the witches. Just before they collided, William jumped off his horse into the air and changed into a manticore mid-fall, reaching the ground in his full form. He went after the centaur leader, Larrus, and the battle began.

Witches were being slashed by the soldiers, and soldiers were overpowered by spells and slashed by the centaurs. Amara used her power to protect rather than to fight.

At one moment, a soldier came up behind Agnes while she was fighting another; he lifted his sword and tried to attack her. Amara saw this happening and, in the heat of the moment, picked up a sword lying nearby with a spell and threw it at him. It stabbed him right through the heart, and he fell to his knees. Amara stood there, shocked at what she had just done, but she didn't feel disgusted with herself; she only felt power. When she turned, she saw Henry standing behind her; he stumbled back. He couldn't believe what he had just seen.

"Please, Amara, you have to leave. This isn't you," he shouted, taking off his helmet and throwing it on the ground.

"Oh, but I think it is," she said, looking at her hands. It was as if this kill had blackened her heart a little bit. Henry tried to come closer to her amidst all the chaos, but before he could make it, Aiden appeared between them, staring at Henry.

"This is all your fault. This is not her. This is not who she is," Henry shouted.

"Oh yes, it is. You just don't want her to be like this. You want her weak and dependent on you. I want her strong, powerful, not dependent on anyone."

Henry grew angry and drew his sword; Aiden pushed Amara to the side and drew his own sword. In their fight, the hatred between them was palpable. They had never even spoken before today, but they shared something in common: their devotion to Amara. They were both good swordsmen, but Aiden had the advantage over Henry. He had trained from a young age.

Henry struggled to defend himself when suddenly Aiden slashed his face, causing Henry to drop his sword. He touched his face, blood pouring down his cheek.

Suddenly, he felt a pain in his bones. He could physically feel the blood in his veins. He bent over and started to squirm. He was changing. Aiden took a few steps back. This was different from when Amara changed. Her transformation had been beautiful, but Henry's was different. Dangerous.

Aiden stood there and watched as Henry transformed into a manticore. He stood tall, ready to attack. Aiden created a fireball in his hand and threw it at him, but manticores are unbelievably fast, so Henry dodged the fire, attacking Aiden straight away.

Aiden hit the ground and Henry jumped on top of him. He had Aiden by the wrists, preventing him from moving or protecting himself. For the first time in his life, Henry was ready to kill, to take a life, but before he could, another manticore attacked him, causing Henry to release Aiden.

The two beasts were tangled together, fighting. When they separated, they looked at each other. Henry didn't know who this was until he looked it in the eyes. He could hear its thoughts; it was Amara. He was shocked; he didn't know she could change, nor why she had attacked him to save Aiden.

They growled at each other while Amara stood up and walked over to Aiden. Henry glanced at her, turned away, and began to fight others. Amara lay down, Aiden picked up his sword and jumped onto her back. Together, they fought against the soldiers, tearing them to pieces, slashing them. Witches and centaurs were overpowering the King's army, and he could see it. His general looked at him in his manticore form. William nodded his head, and the general signalled for his soldiers to fall back. They knew they were not going to win this fight.

They hadn't expected the centaurs, and it threw them off. They had to regroup and find more allies before attacking again. The witches won. Well, at least this round.

Over two hundred soldiers and forty witches were dead. Agnes ordered the surviving witches to retrieve the bodies so they could bury them. When they arrived at the Black Mansion, Amara returned to her human form.

She could see the anger in Agnes's face.

"How dare you turn? Didn't I tell you how unnatural it is?" screamed Agnes.

"She saved my life by doing that, Mother," Aiden jumped in to defend her.

Agnes was frustrated but also grateful that her son was unharmed. She left them alone and exited the room.

Amara was tending to Aiden, who had scratches all over his face from Henry. She was cleaning his wounds when he grabbed her right hand.

"Thank you for what you did on the field," said Aiden.

"I know it wasn't easy."

"I didn't want to hurt him, but when he attacked you, I couldn't help myself. I felt like I could harm him—for you."

He kissed her, his hand slowly playing with her hair.

"What is it about you that would make me jump through fire?" He tucked her hair behind her ear.

"What is it about you that I would fight my own family just to protect you?" she replied.

This wasn't only an attraction or lust anymore; they were falling for each other. They were the same but different. After their kiss, they just sat there, holding each other and talking.

Larrus walked up to Agnes while she was standing in front of the Black Mansion.

"Thank you for coming here to help us fight," she said.

Larrus smiled. "You know I would do anything for you."

They spoke for a while. They both knew this wasn't the end. They knew William would attack again, and this time he would come more prepared.

"What of the girl? She is his daughter, after all. Do you trust her?" he asked.

"I do. Amara might be the King's daughter, but she knows she belongs here, with us."

"Does she know everything? Did you share your secrets with her?"

"Not everything, and you know better than anyone that there is one secret neither she nor Aiden can ever know," Agnes replied.

They sat for a little while longer, and after Agnes went back inside the mansion, Larrus returned to the forest to join his own for the night.

"How do you know him? Why did he help us?" Amara appeared behind Agnes as she was walking through the house.

"Where is Aiden?" Agnes tried to change the topic.

"Asleep. Now, how do you know a tribe of centaurs who are willing to fight for us? What aren't you telling me?"

Agnes took a deep breath and pressed her lips together as she exhaled.

"Larrus and I…" She paused for a few seconds, then continued. "We have known each other for a very long time."

Amara sat down, signalling to Agnes to sit next to her and tell her the story, and so Agnes did.

She told Amara that when her grandfather attacked all the witches in the kingdom in the winter of 1968, she was only seven years old. Her mother used a protection spell to hide her while they fought the King. She was hidden in the closet, and if anyone opened it, they wouldn't see her, as she was cloaked. Agnes was there for two days before she dared to leave the closet. She ventured into the woods, and on her way, she saw many dead bodies, mostly witches, including her mother.

She wasn't able to keep track of how many she had seen. She was cold and alone and didn't know where she should go. She was so hungry that she could barely keep walking. Her legs were so weak that after a while, she collapsed onto the ground. She sat there in the snow, freezing, shivering. Her lips started to turn blue, and she was passing out on and off.

When suddenly, she heard a noise behind her. She turned and saw a strange creature she had never seen before. It was Larrus. She could tell he was a couple of years older than her. He was half human, half horse. The last thing she remembered was this creature scooping her up and carrying her somewhere, and then she passed out completely. When she woke up after two days, she was in a cabin with a furry blanket on top of her. She could hear a fire crackling nearby.

She sat up in the bed and looked around. She saw a similar creature to the one in the forest, only bigger—much bigger. It was Larrus' mother. They saved her. He carried her to his home, and he and his mother took care of her for years after they learned her story. They grew up together. He was like a brother to her.

Centaurs also disliked humans because of the way they treated them. They thought of centaurs as beasts, which was a bit rich considering what the royal family was like.

"I am sorry this happened to you and your family. So, you and Larrus have never… you know. You were never together?" asked Amara.

Agnes chuckled. "No, no. I thought we might be one day, but I knew I had a bigger calling. I left their home when I was 15 and found my own little coven far away from here. That's where I met Aiden's father."

"What happened to him? And to the coven?"

"Aiden's father died in an accident, and the coven didn't want to come here with me to take what was rightfully mine, so I took Aiden, and I left."

Amara couldn't believe the story. Agnes had gone through so much at such a young age. She felt sorrow for her. She also felt disgusted with her grandfather. She had never met him, and now she was glad she hadn't. How could her father do the same as he had? She always knew William hated witches and would never let her use her power, but she had never been told the true history behind that hate.

Right then and there, she knew she would not let her family hurt her coven ever again. No matter what it took.

"I know you don't like manticores because of what they have done to you and your family, but it's who I am; it's a part of me," said Amara.

"I know it is. I just can't help but feel this hatred towards them. They ripped my family apart, and you are half the beast that caused my family's death—that caused all the pain."

"I would never hurt you or anyone else in our coven. I am here to help you. I can be a manticore that protects us all."

Agnes took a while to think about this, but even she had to admit that if Amara practised both—being a manticore and mastering her spells—no one would ever dare to try to hurt them again.

"Very well. You can practise your other side as well, but witchcraft always comes first," said Agnes before she left to go to her room to get some sleep.

Amara was pleased with how the conversation had gone between them. She felt much closer to Agnes now. She was happy she could practise her shapeshifting and her fighting skills. At the end of the day, she was a hybrid.

She was part witch and part manticore, and she wanted to be the best in both. Once she was, she would be able to become the leader she was born to be. She would unite humans and witches, and they would all live in peace. This was her destiny. At least, she thought it was.

CHAPTER 12

The Hunter

The day after the battle, Henry woke up feeling unbelievably sore but also happy. He had changed.

He still didn't understand how. He hadn't had a powerful thought in his mind when it happened. He knew he wanted to do it again as soon as possible. He got up, got dressed, and went to see his uncle. He found him in the library, reading everything there was on witches. He hoped he could find something that would help them in the next battle, which he was already planning out of anger.

William was a very proud man. He hated them now more than ever for embarrassing him in front of his army. He also felt anger towards Amara for the way he had seen her on the battlefield. He was ashamed of his daughter.

"Uncle, can I speak to you?" Henry interrupted William's deep thoughts.

"Hmm, uncle. I never thought I would be called that, but it has a nice ring to it. What can I help you with?"

"Yesterday, during the battle, I changed for the first time, and I was wondering if we could talk about what it means to be a manticore. I still don't really understand it."

William smiled and asked Henry to sit in the chair opposite him. He told Henry he still remembered the first time that he and Peter had changed. They had done it together, as brothers should. He remembered the power and the freedom he had felt. Henry told him these were the emotions he recalled.

"Being a manticore is all about strength, pride, and family. We can do so much. You'll see," said William.

Henry smiled. "Can you tell me something about my father?"

William looked at the ground and then back at Henry. He told him that he loved his brother. Peter was kind, compassionate, and funny. He missed him every day and wished he could see Henry as the great young man he had become.

"I know what everyone says, Henry, but I promise you that I didn't harm your father. I wouldn't do that to my own brother, to my own blood."

Henry thought to himself that he actually believed him, given the way he spoke about his father. He didn't think William had anything to do with his murder.

"You look exactly like him when he was younger, you know."

"Do I?" asked Henry.

"Yes, you do, and I can also see the similarities in your personalities. It's like he came back to me through you."

Henry started to pace around the room, then said, "I want to find the person who murdered my father. I have to."

"Okay, let's say you find them. Then what? What will you do then?" asked William.

"I will make them pay for what they have done."

"Then let me help you. Let's find this murderer together, as a family."

This was the first time either of them had felt any type of connection between them.

William never admitted it, but he had always wanted a son. Yes, he loved his daughter, but she wasn't who he thought she was. He couldn't stand to look at her as a witch. He had been raised to hate them. It was all he knew.

"I know you want Amara back, but you should make peace with the fact that she will stay loyal to them. I did," said William.

"I think I am starting to," Henry replied as he stood up and left the library.

He took Pearl and went into the forest. He wanted to be alone in nature. He lay down under a tree and just watched the sky. He was thinking about how beautiful this place was and how lucky he was to have met Amara and found his true self. His real home. He felt sad that she had decided to betray them, but now he could try to forget about her— maybe even find someone new, someone truly worthy of his love.

"Hi," Henry heard behind him, and when he turned, he saw Eleanor.

"You have a way of sneaking up on me."

Eleanor smiled and sat down beside him. She didn't say anything; she was simply admiring the beauty of the Gulrose Forest.

He looked at her and asked, "Eleanor, were you at the battlefield yesterday?"

"You can call me El."

He laughed, noticing how she avoided answering his question. He looked at her, seeing her biting her lips. Was she nervous to answer?

"Alright, El," he chuckled, "it's okay—you don't have to tell me if you don't want to."

"No, I wasn't there. My father didn't allow me to come, even though I wanted to," she finally answered.

"Your father? Who is your father?"

"Ares. He is the leader of our coven. We came here to help Agnes."

Eleanor didn't look pleased to be here; in fact, she seemed a bit upset about it.

She said it looked different now, after all these years. It felt different. She didn't want to stay. They had built a new home somewhere else. This was just a strange place to her now.

"Oh look, a faded flower," she said, putting her hands around it. She closed her eyes and took a breath. "Stiga vaxa, stiga vaxa."

The flower began to slowly glow and grow. Henry smiled. This was a spell he had seen Amara use when they came to rescue her—when she had broken his heart by staying with the enemy. He pushed the thought of Amara out of his mind and said to Eleanor,

"I enjoy talking to you. Maybe we could do it more often?"

"I would like that. Shall we meet here again tomorrow?" she replied, then tried to stand up but stumbled and fell back down.

"Whoa, are you alright?" Henry caught her before she hit the ground.

"Yes, I'm fine. Thank you. Just a bit tired."

He helped her up, and after making sure she was truly alright, they said their goodbyes. Eleanor went back to the mansion, and Henry returned to the castle, where he ran into Arthur.

He looked a bit worried, so Henry asked if there was something he wanted to talk about. Arthur gave him a concerned look and said he'd given it a lot of thought. He loved the kingdom, but he didn't feel he belonged here. He wanted to return to London, to his old life.

Henry felt sad that his mentor was leaving him, but with

everything going on, it was probably a wise decision.

"Arthur, I want you to help me convince my mum to leave with you," Henry said.

Arthur nodded. "You know she won't like that."

"I know, but she isn't safe here. She's not a manticore, a witch, or a knight, and I have a feeling that the first battle was only the beginning of something far worse, something more dangerous. If she stays, she could get hurt."

They went together to Theodore first, asking if he could send both of them back to London. He said he wasn't sure he had enough power to do it, but he would try his best. After speaking with him, they went to see Mary. She didn't want to hear it; she didn't want to leave her son.

"Mum, I can't protect you here. You'll be safe in London, and once this is all over, I'll send for you, I promise. Then we'll live here together."

"You look just like your father," she said.

"Mum, please, the next battle will be much worse than the first, and if we fail, they will take over this castle and I don't know what they will do to you," Henry pleaded.

She thought about it for a while and finally agreed. She wasn't any help here. Though she didn't want to leave Henry, she knew he wasn't going to come with her no matter what. And so, it was decided. They didn't know when the next battle would happen, so they planned to leave that night.

Arthur and Mary said their goodbyes to Catherine, Theodore, and the King. When it came time to say goodbye to Henry, Mary hugged him tightly, tears streaming down her face. She made him promise he would come back for her as soon as he could and that he would try to stay safe. Henry hugged her back, kissing her cheek. Theodore took his position and began chanting the spell to send them to London.

"Ta mig härifrån, ta mig härifrån."

Mary smiled at Henry, a final tear falling down her face—then they were gone.

Henry closed his eyes. Sending his mother away was heartbreaking, but he knew it was the only way to keep her safe.

"Henry, come with me," William said suddenly.

Henry wiped away his tears and followed his uncle. They arrived at the library, where William pulled out a book.

He had once heard a story, long ago, about a witch hunter. He wasn't sure if it was real or just a legend, but he knew that if it was true, it could possibly solve their problem. He handed the book to Henry and began to tell him the tale.

Before William's father attacked and killed most of the witches, there was another who fought against them and their dark ways. His name was Elias. Though he was human, he possessed extraordinary strength and knowledge. He became a legend, defeating and killing hundreds of witches. Elias even had his own group of trained witch hunters. Together, they travelled the world, helping villages plagued by witches who stole children for their sacrifices and terrorised entire communities.

"If we can find him and convince him and his group to fight alongside us," William explained, "we could rid ourselves of the witches for good. These hunters are strong and fast. Their weapons leave witches with no chance. It might be our only hope, Henry. Will you come with me to find him?"

Henry hesitated. "If we find him and bring him back with us… what will happen to Amara?"

William's gaze softened. "I would never harm my own daughter, even if I don't agree with her choices. She'll be safe. I'll make sure of it."

"And Aiden?"

William looked at him carefully. "What would you like to happen to him?"

"I want him dead," Henry said, looking at William with an intense, unsettling gaze.

William sat down and poured himself a glass of wine.

"Then it shall be done."

"In that case, I'll come with you,"

William smiled, feeling a swell of pride in the man Henry had become. They informed Theodore of their plans, quickly gathered a few essentials, and set off.

Elias and his hunters were said to live southwest of the Gulrose Kingdom, on the far side of Mörkdimma. With an uninterrupted journey, it would take them about two full days to travel. Time was critical; they couldn't risk the witches launching another attack and seizing the castle while they were away.

During the journey, they had plenty of time to talk about Peter. William shared stories from their youth, moments Henry had never heard of before. Henry noticed the sorrow in William's eyes as he spoke of his brother, and now, more than ever, he felt certain that his uncle was not responsible for his father's death.

William told Henry that Peter had always been gentle, even as a child. He would stop to help the less fortunate, always taking time for the people in their kingdom. In some ways, it had been a relief when Peter won the contest to become the next king; William knew people loved and respected him. Peter was a true leader.

Their father, Leopold, was different. William recalled how his father's hatred for magic had begun to fester when he and Peter were only ten. Their mother, a compassionate and open-hearted queen, had befriended a witch who lived near the kingdom.

The two women had become close, like sisters. But one day, while walking alone in the woods to visit her friend, their mother encountered a passing wizard. He saw a beautiful queen alone, and when she refused his advances, he assaulted and killed her. Leopold learned that this wizard was kin to his wife's friend, the witch, and from that day forward, he vowed to purge his land of all magic.

When the boys were twelve, Leopold waged war against the witches, and won. Since then, they believed there were no more witches in the kingdom; the ones who had survived had fled. Or so they thought. Henry was stunned. What had happened to his grandmother was horrific, and he could understand, on some level, why his grandfather had been driven to such extremes. He knew that if anyone ever harmed Amara, he would seek the same vengeance.

As the day's journey wore on, they finally decided to camp in the woods for the night. Setting up a small campfire, they sat around its warm glow, sharing food and more stories. Henry couldn't stop smiling as he listened to William's stories about his father. Every story painted Peter as an honourable, kind man, and Henry felt a deep pride in being his son.

"Do you think the witches murdered my father?" Henry finally asked.

"I'm not sure. I've wondered about it many times, but I always believed that if they'd wanted revenge, they would have tried to kill me as well."

Henry nodded. "I have my father's diaries. I've read parts of them, and he mentioned several times that he felt like someone was following him before he was murdered."

William raised an eyebrow. "Did he say who it was?"

"No," Henry replied, "but I didn't go through all of it. Once we return, I'll read more. Maybe I'll find something that points to someone."

William hesitated, then asked, "Do you think... after you're done with them, I could read them as well?"

Henry smiled. "I think that would be fine."

Their bond had grown since the battle, strengthened by their shared love for Peter. They settled in for the night, and at dawn, they set off again, determined to reach their destination.

After nearly two more days, they arrived at Dodblomma. It looked very different from the Gulrose Kingdom. It was a small village in a small kingdom. It appeared very poor and dirty, full of people working their way through life. Many small children ran around with fake swords, play fighting.

They walked around the village for a while. Eventually, they approached an older woman, asking her if she knew someone by the name of Elias. The woman didn't speak; she only pointed at a house on top of a hill and walked away.

Henry and William looked at the house and started walking towards it.

When they reached the hill, they saw a large house, almost a mansion. It wasn't in the best condition. It was dark grey, and most of the windows were covered. They walked up to the door and knocked four times.

They waited for a while, and then the door swung open. A young girl with blonde hair stood there.

"Can I help you?" she asked.

"My name is William. I am the King of the Gulrose Kingdom, and we have come to speak to Elias."

"Wait here," she said and shut the door.

They exchanged confused looks and waited. After a few minutes, she returned and invited them in. She led them into a great chamber and told them to sit down while they waited. Elias would be with them shortly. Then, she left.

After a few minutes, a tall, sturdy man entered the room. William and Henry stood up and introduced themselves.

"I am Elias. What can I do for you, Your Majesty?"

"We need your help. We have a bit of a witch problem in my kingdom," said William.

Elias looked at them long and hard. They could see he was deciding whether to help them or turn them away. After a while, he asked William to tell him more. He seemed intrigued. William explained everything that had happened to them and what the witches had done to his daughter. He told Elias they needed his help because, even with their physical power, they were not strong enough to defeat the witches, especially with the centaurs on their side.

"Now, why would I travel that far and help you?" asked Elias.

"We have gold. Lots of it," said William.

"Yes, yes. Gold would be fine, but it's not really a fair payment for our services."

"Anything you want, as long as you help us to be rid of all of them," said William.

"You mentioned their leader? Agnes?"

"Yes. Do you know her?" asked Henry.

"I do. Come with me."

They followed Elias down the stairs to the basement. It was a large room filled with all kinds of weapons. They kept walking and arrived in another room. This one was large and full of collectibles. It contained various artifacts that had belonged to witches the hunters had killed.

There were wands, elixirs, and much more.

Elias took a key out of his jacket and opened a small gold chest. Inside were five empty spaces in rectangular shapes. Elias explained that there were five pendants scattered around the world: Amber, Navy, Maroon, Lilac, and Emerald. Each had a unique power. Amber could control animals and allow the wearer to speak to them. Navy could make the wearer invisible. Maroon could stop time. Lilac could give the wearer the power to read anyone's thoughts. Emerald could absorb magical power. He explained that if they collected all five, they would become unstoppable. Once they had all five, the pendants could be joined into one, making the wearer the master of all species in Mörkdimma. However, they needed a powerful witch to cast a spell to unite them and enchant the artifact so a human could use it. That's why he wanted Agnes. She came from an old and powerful magical family. Her ancestors had created the pendants, and only someone from her bloodline could unite them. She was also the only person who could tell them where the rest were.

"Lilian!" shouted Elias.

A dark-haired, beautiful girl walked in. Elias told her what he had just learned. He never made any decisions involving his hunters without consulting her. She was the leader of the team. She listened to the story and took a moment to think about it. Then, she agreed to help them. She explained that they had 17 hunters who had eliminated over 300 witches, which was how they had retrieved all the artifacts on display. They agreed that Amara would not be harmed and would be safely returned to the king.

William and Henry didn't care what happened to Agnes. She had Amara, and that was all they cared about. Elias said he would prepare his hunters and arrive in the Gulrose Kingdom in one week. William asked Henry to prepare the horses and told him he would be right behind him. Henry did as he was told and waited for William. After a while, William returned, and they set off on their journey back to the kingdom.

CHAPTER 13

The Forbidden Love

While Agnes went into the woods to discuss the next steps with Larrus, Amara and Aiden were searching for the pendant inside the mansion.

They started in her room, then moved to the loft, and finally descended into the basement, where all the grimoires and other magical items were kept. They went through every small and large chest, looking for any sign of the pendant. Eventually, Amara found a black chest that was locked.

"Why is this one locked?" she asked.

Aiden came closer and examined the chest. "Hm, I don't know. I've never seen that before."

He placed his hand on it and began to chant a spell.

"Oppna avsloja, oppna avsloja," he muttered, then paused and gasped. "This isn't locked with just a key, Mar. Even if we found it, we wouldn't be able to open it."

"Why not? What is it? What do we need?"

"Only the person who enchanted this can open it," he replied.

"It was your mother, I know it."

"We might not need her, just a drop of her blood."

Amara tilted her head. "Can't we use your blood then? You're her son."

"No, this is a different type of spell; it's not blood magic. Only she can open it, but if I have a drop of her blood, I think I could confuse it with another spell, and maybe, just maybe, it will open."

They both knew that getting Agnes's blood would be hard, if not impossible. They needed to come up with a plan, and they had to do it quickly.

When they left the basement, Agnes was back at the mansion. She called them both into the great hall. Once they were inside, she told them she had spoken to Larrus, and they would attack the King and all those who followed him.

Amara took a few steps forward. "I don't understand. I thought when we won the battle, that was it. Why would we want to attack?"

"Don't be naive, Amara. They will attack again and again—until they win, or until there is no human left alive to fight," said Agnes.

"I thought you wanted to reunite the witches. That's why I'm here—to help you do that. But I won't wage war against my father, my mother, or Henry. I won't do it."

"Do you know what your father thinks of you? And your mother? They think you're a freak. A sin against nature. A filthy hybrid. That's what they think of you. Even your precious Henry," said Agnes.

Amara had tears in her eyes; surely that wasn't what they thought of her. But then she started to think about it. Her father had shielded her from everything. Everything that was magical, he had never even told her she was a manticore. He had never shown her any love or affection.

Her mother had left her when she was barely an hour old. Yes, she had gone to find the pendant, but it now seemed it was too easy for her to leave her. And Henry? What if he had made up the whole story of them being related because he didn't want to be with her? He had said during the battle that what he saw wasn't her, that he didn't like her like this. He didn't like who she was; he didn't like her power.

She slowly started to believe Agnes's words. It hurt her; it broke her. She ran from the mansion and into the woods. She ran and ran, hearing all the bad thoughts in her head, then before she knew it, she shapeshifted. She was running through the woods on all fours when suddenly she stopped. She listened to the wind and the footsteps behind her. She turned and saw another manticore. It wasn't Henry or her father. She didn't know who it was. It looked at her, and it seemed like it was also trying to figure out who Amara was; then it turned and ran away.

Just as Amara was about to run after it, Aiden appeared in front of her, looking at her with a faded smile, holding a coat in his hands. Amara changed back to her human form and took the coat, then sat down on the ground, sobbing. Aiden sat next to her and just held her, without saying a word.

"Why does no one love me?" she asked.

"That's not true. She didn't mean what she said."

"She's right. If you think about it, they all abandoned me when things got hard. I don't have anyone."

"You have me. I would do anything for you; you know that. I will always be there for you."

Amara looked up at him and smiled. She hoped he was telling the truth, but she still didn't know if she could completely trust him.

It was getting dark, so they went back to the mansion. Amara couldn't stop thinking about the manticore she had seen earlier. She had never seen him before. She could tell he was male, but she couldn't hear his thoughts.

When they arrived, Aiden went to his room to go to sleep, and Amara went to the library. She wanted to know more about her kind.

She found a book about mythical creatures and read through it until she found a section dedicated to them. According to the book, it all started with her family; they were royalty in the human world but also in the world of manticores. They were cursed, and the only other way to become one if you were not of their blood was to be stung by one. She learned about their strength, some of which she had already experienced.

What she didn't know was that they could jump unbelievably far with only one leap. She also didn't know that manticores could shoot poisonous darts from their tails. Once the poison entered your body, there was no antidote, and you would die within an hour. It wasn't easy, however, to use this talent. Only an older manticore could usually shoot the poisonous dart correctly.

She kept reading until she fell asleep. She was woken in the middle of the night by strange sounds coming from the basement. She got up and went to see what it was. When she was close, she recognised the voices. It was Agnes and Ares, chanting. She sneaked up behind the wall and watched. She saw them performing a spell she didn't know. She saw a pentagram with candles all around and a piece of paper in the middle. There were two names written on it: William and Henry. Amara kept watching for a while longer, then ran.

She ran to wake Aiden. When he woke up, he was confused by what she was saying. She told him what the enchantments she had heard were and asked if he knew what spell it was, and he did. He told her it was a binding spell. It was used to bind two people, and whatever happened to one would happen to the other.

Amara sat down on the bed next to Aiden. "Why would she want to bind my father and Henry?"

"Maybe because she knows they are the biggest threat, and she will try to eliminate one of them first. What happens to one happens to the other," said Aiden.

Amara's face went pale. "We have to open the chest. I'm sure the pendant is in there."

"And I think I might know how to get her blood," said Aiden.

Their plan was simple. They would train in the morning as they did every day, and when Agnes was near, they would practise throwing spells. When she was close, they would throw a log or something similarly heavy at her, hitting her. As long as there was even one drop of blood on the ground, they could use an extraction spell to bottle it.

Amara let Aiden go back to sleep, and she went to her room.

In the morning, there was a knock on her door. When she invited whoever was on the other side in, she was surprised to see it was Eleanor.

She went to see her because there was something important, she wanted to discuss. Of course, they had seen each other before around the mansion, but they had never really spoken.

"Can I come in?" she asked.

"Yes. Please do," Amara replied as she sat up on her bed.

There was an awkward silence between them before Eleanor told her why she was there.

She wanted Amara to speak to El's father. He didn't want her to go to the battle; she couldn't even go to the first one. She was the only family he had left, and he didn't want anything to happen to her. But she needed to be in the next battle. There was someone she wanted to protect—Henry.

Amara's heart sank a little. She didn't know that El and Henry knew each other or that there was something going on between them. She found herself feeling something she had never felt before: jealousy. She didn't know El well, but now she felt nothing but anger towards her.

She had always thought of herself as someone who wasn't capable of hate or of having thoughts of hurting someone. It was as if this place and these people had turned her into something she didn't think she was.

Amara agreed and promised El that she would speak to Ares. In her mind, if Eleanor got killed during the battle, she would not have Henry. Amara just needed to make sure El didn't survive.

Eleanor thanked her and left the room. Amara got dressed and went to speak to Ares. After a long conversation, he agreed. Amara was supposed to be their leader, so it didn't take much convincing.

After she left Ares, she met with Aiden outside to start their training and to try to succeed with their plan. They practised some new spells from the dark spellbook. Amara realised she hadn't been as helpful in the first battle as she would have liked to be. She had to shapeshift to protect Aiden, and this time around, she wanted to be able to protect anyone she wanted with her magic as well.

Agnes walked outside on her way to Larrus to plan their attack. She stopped for a while to watch Aiden and Amara, enjoying the sight of them practising. It made her feel proud of them.

Aiden looked at Amara long and deep, and she understood. It was now or never. Aiden threw a log lying nearby at Amara, and she dodged it, pretending her intention was to throw it back at Aiden, but it hit Agnes instead. Agnes screamed and fell to the ground, her nose bleeding and drops of blood dripping onto the ground.

Amara ran to Agnes, pretending to be concerned. Aiden did the same. They kept apologising profusely, but Agnes assured them it was an accident and that accidents could happen during training. She went inside to clean herself up, telling them to continue.

When she was gone, Aiden ran to the place where Agnes had bled. He took out a little vial and started to chant,

"Flyggaflytande binda."

The small drops of blood began to lift from the ground and form into one. Aiden positioned the bottle under the blood drop, and it fell inside. He bottled it up then put it in his pocket.

When Agnes came back out, they were already training again; she did not suspect a thing. As soon as she left, they ran inside, straight into the basement.

Before they tried to open the chest, Aiden stopped.

"What is it?" Amara asked.

"If we can open it and the pendant is, in fact, there, we can't just leave it empty."

Amara thought this was a good point. If Agnes came down here to look at it and saw it was empty, she would know it was them. The fake pendant Agnes had made and left in London couldn't be used, as she always wore it around her neck.

"Can you make a replica of this, like your mother did?" Amara asked.

"I've never done it, but I guess I could if I have the right spell."

So that was it for now; the chest and the mystery inside would remain out of their reach until Aiden could figure out how to create another replica.

They left the basement and went into Amara's room.

"We have to preserve her blood. I don't know how long it will take me," said Aiden.

It was decided that the vial would stay in Amara's room and would be spell-protected. They put it in her musical jewellery chest and enchanted it. If anyone but Amara were to open this chest, they would not see the vial.

Amara looked at Aiden, smiled, and held his hand. Aiden pulled away, leaving Amara confused.

"Why did you do that?" she asked.

"Amara, we can't be together like this; you know that."

"Why not? We care for each other, and we are a great team."

"You know mother wouldn't allow it. We are siblings in her eyes, and it wouldn't be the best for the coven," he said.

Amara didn't care. He wasn't her biological brother, not even a stepbrother. She was born of her mother and father, who had nothing to do with Agnes or Aiden. The only way Agnes was involved was the potion that helped her mother conceive and gave Amara magical powers. She came closer to Aiden, who closed his eyes. She could see he was fighting this with every fibre of his being. There was no point; Amara was his weakness, his muse.

She came closer, put her hand on his face, and kissed him. At first, he just stood there, not moving, but after a few seconds, he grabbed her and kissed her back.

Yes, Amara had won again. She was getting what she wanted. She wasn't even sure she wanted Aiden, but she knew that when he denied her, it was precisely that which made her want him more.

CHAPTER 14

Imprisonment

Henry woke up feeling tired. The two days' travel to the village in the Dodblomma Kingdom had exhausted him, and even more so on the way back. All he wanted to do was go back to bed, but he knew there would be enough time for that after the witches were gone.

He got dressed and made his way into the forest. He was hoping for a good training session, but he was also hoping to see El. He had not seen her in over three days, and he found himself thinking about her quite a lot. When he arrived, he took out his sword and looked around, but she wasn't there. He felt disappointed and started his training. He could sense he was getting better; his feet were planted more firmly on the ground, and he didn't trip as much as he used to. After a little while, he heard footsteps approaching, and his smile faded when he realised it was not Eleanor.

It was the King's soldiers. He had never seen them in these parts before. They exchanged a few words, and Henry asked them what they were doing there. The soldiers told him they were looking for witches.

Henry's eyebrows raised.

"Why are you looking them, exactly?"

"By the King's order. Any witch found in these woods is to be taken back to the castle, put in the dungeon, and then executed," one of the soldiers replied before saying goodbye to Henry and leaving.

Henry couldn't believe that William hadn't told him about this new order. He knew he would need to speak to him when he was back in the castle to find out what was going on.

Another set of footsteps could be heard behind him. Henry thought it might be another group of soldiers, so he shouted,

"No witches here, boys, just me."

"Well, that is a shame, but I guess you will have to do."

He turned and saw her—El. She was laughing. Henry had a big smile on his face before he realised, she shouldn't be here. He told her what he had just learned and that she needed to leave the forest. She wasn't safe there; the soldiers could come back at any moment. He kept looking around as he moved closer to her. El laughed and told him not to worry about her. She could protect herself against some basic soldiers.

Henry looked around nervously. He didn't see any soldiers as far as his eyes could see, but he still felt slightly uneasy. El sat down and started to hum.

"What song is that?" he asked.

She smiled and said, "Oh, no song, just this silly melody in my head."

He sat down next to her and started to pull weeds from the ground. Eleanor knew he was nervous when she was near him; she felt the same way, only she was better at hiding it. She told Henry that her father had allowed her to be in the next battle thanks to Amara.

"Amara? What do you mean?"

"Yes, she was great. She convinced him to let me fight."

Henry's eyes squinted. "But why would she want to put you in harm's way? That doesn't make sense."

"No, no, it's not like that. I asked her to speak to my father. I want to fight. I want to fight for my family. I can't just hide while they challenge the King's army."

Henry suddenly understood why she wanted to be in the battle. She had the same reasons he had; they were just on two different sides of this. They both fought for their families and for what they thought was right. He couldn't believe that both women he cared about were on opposite sides. It would be much easier if they all fought for the same cause—or better yet, if none of them had to fight at all.

He wished he could just come here, meet El, and see if there was a future for them. He knew he could never have any future with Amara, even if there was no hate between humans and witches. They would always be cousins.

Eleanor could see that his head was full of doubts and thoughts. She looked at him, smiled, and put her hand on his. He looked down and then back up at her, also smiling. She moved closer, and so did he; just before their lips touched, he put his other hand behind her neck. This was different from when he kissed Amara. This felt stronger, more intense—more real. It was as if his gut was telling him this was supposed to happen.

After they kissed, they laid down, with El lying in Henry's arms, enjoying the quiet around them. It was cold at the start of December, but they didn't care. They just wanted to be there, in that moment, together.

Their romantic time was interrupted by little white snowflakes falling from the sky. Eleanor smiled and lifted her hands in the air, trying to catch them. Henry chuckled, looking at her lips. How lucky he was to be there with this beautiful girl who wanted to be there with him.

Eleanor asked Henry to bring some wood so they could make a fire. He stood up, gathered a few logs that were lying around, and arranged them.

"Okay, how are we going to make a fire? I don't have any matches," he said.

Eleanor chuckled and lifted her hand. She whispered something that Henry couldn't quite understand and knelt in front of the logs. A small ball of fire appeared in her hand; she smiled and, with one breath, sent the ball of fire into the middle of the logs, starting a fire.

Henry's eyes widened, and his mouth slightly opened. While he kept staring at the fire in amazement, he didn't notice that Eleanor's nose had started to bleed. She quickly wiped it away and got close to Henry.

They cuddled up in front of the fire and shared stories from their childhood. For the first time since arriving, Henry felt truly happy.

Before it got completely dark, El had to go back to meet her father. She kissed Henry goodbye and promised she would meet him there the next day, at the same time.

On the way back to the castle, Henry couldn't help but smile. He thought about El's lips and the way she touched him. He was completely smitten with her. Finally, it seemed like Amara didn't have a place in his heart like she used to. He knew he would always care about her, but they could never be the way they once were. Too much had happened.

When he arrived at the castle, he changed his clothes and went to see his uncle. He had a lot of questions about this new order. When he found him, he talked about what the soldiers had told him in the forest, and the King confirmed that it was true. He would no longer act decently towards the witches.

The hunters would arrive in four days, but until then, any witch seen in the kingdom would be arrested and executed in front of all the people in Gulrose. The King wanted to demonstrate power and strength; he wanted to ensure that no one would ever doubt him again.

"Come, they actually caught one just before you arrived."

Henry felt uneasy as he followed William into the dungeons. It was dark and wet, smelling like old meat. He could hear and see rats running around.

When they arrived at the cell where the witch was held, Henry stood frozen. It was Eleanor, passed out on the ground, not moving.

His fingers curled into his palm, forming a fist as he stepped closer.

"Eleanor!" he whispered.

"You know this wicked thing?" the King asked.

"Um, yes, our paths crossed a couple of times," Henry said, cowardly stepping back.

William could tell there was more to Henry's expression. He came closer to Henry and whispered in his ear, "Just remember who you are, who your father was, and what we stand and fight for."

Then he took a long look at Henry, turned around, and left the dungeon. Henry also turned to leave but then hesitated. He looked at Eleanor, lying there, and knew he had to do something to get her out. He ran to get his horse and sped away from the castle, his destination? The Black Mansion.

It took him some time to arrive, but when he did, he did not hesitate to knock on the door. A witch he had never met before opened it. She knew who Henry was; he and William were well known by all the witches in this house. Henry urged her to get El's father. She closed the door in his face, and he stood there, hoping he would come and talk to him. When the door opened, a tall man with an angry expression stood before him.

"What do you want?"

Henry, out of breath, muttered, "The King has your daughter. He has Eleanor."

Ares looked at Henry with disgust.

"I should have known when she didn't come home on time. What have you done to her?"

"I have not done anything to her, sir, I promise. I like her; I care about her. That's why I am here."

"How do you even know her? My daughter knows better than to mix with the likes of you."

"We met a few times in the woods, and we just talked. Please, I can't get her out; it has to be you," pleaded Henry.

Before Ares could say anything else, a loud "no" sounded behind him. When he turned, he saw Amara.

"What? What do you mean no?" asked Ares.

""We can't risk any more lives trying to save one witch if we are to win against my father."

"Amara, please," said Henry.

Amara smirked, "So, you found a new one? That was quick."

"This has nothing to do with you and me. Please, you have to help El."

"El? El. Hmm, that's an adorable nickname," she said.

Ares looked at her with desperation in his eyes. "Please, Amara, let me go and save my daughter. I can't lose her too."

Amara took a moment to think and then said, "Fine, but you're on your own. I will not allow any other witch to go to that castle and get killed."

Henry offered to take Ares with him on Pearl, and he reluctantly accepted. Pearl was running as fast as she could, and after a while, they arrived near the castle. Before they could devise a plan to save Eleanor, they heard a commotion coming from the courtyard. They made their way there, trying not to be noticed. They kept their heads down, their hoods up, and their eyes on the ground. When they finally made it in front of the crowd, what they saw made them gasp. Eleanor was bound to a stake, blindfolded. Henry and Ares stood there in shock as the King began to speak.

"Today, we will prove we are stronger than these magical wretches. They will never have this kingdom, and they will never be leaders! Archers! Aim," he shouted.

"I have to do something," said Ares, looking around manically.

"But what? They will kill you too."

"I don't care. That is my daughter, Henry."

Henry could see Ares forming a ball of fire in his hands, and before the King could give the order to shoot, Ares hurled the fireball at the archers.

"Another one! Get him!" William shouted, pointing at Ares.

Filled with anger at the abduction of his daughter, Ares attacked anyone who came at him.

He was a powerful wizard—not as powerful as Agnes or Amara, but still formidable. While he fought the soldiers, Henry seized the chance to try to help Eleanor, but before he could reach her, someone grabbed his arm. It was William.

"What are you doing?"

"This is not right, Uncle. This isn't fair. She is just a girl."

"If you help her, you are betraying your family. But most importantly, you are betraying your father."

Henry stood there, contemplating what to do. Of course, he knew the right thing was to save Eleanor, but he didn't know how his uncle would react; he would probably stop him before he could even reach her.

"They killed your father; I am sure of it."

Henry took a few steps back and turned around. He saw Ares now on the ground, overpowered by the soldiers. They took him and tied him next to Eleanor, also blindfolding him.

"Eleanor?" Ares whispered.

"Dad?"

"Yes, I am here. I am so sorry. I failed you. I am so sorry," he cried.

"It's okay, dad. You are here with me now," she sobbed.

Henry watched as they tried to reach for each other.

"FIRE!" shouted William.

Arrows flew and struck both Ares and Eleanor in their chests at the same time. They gasped as if taking their last breaths, and their heads slowly dropped.

Henry gulped; tears flooded his eyes. He fell to his knees and closed his eyes, holding his stomach as if he had just been stabbed. It was too much for him to bear; he couldn't look at them—especially not at Eleanor. After a moment, he stood up and looked around. Everyone around him cheered, including his uncle.

All the noise was muted in his head. He began to frantically look around, breathing heavily. His head was spinning, and he felt like he was about to pass out.

He ran back to his room, collapsing onto the ground, sobbing. His uncle had just killed El—his sweet, innocent El. Anger surged within him, directed at his uncle, but then he redirected that anger toward someone else: someone who had the chance to help both El and Ares but had refused to act—Amara. He stood up and started calling her name, wiping away his tears. He hoped she would appear, but she didn't. After a few minutes, he gave up. He knew he couldn't confront his uncle; he was even more dangerous than before. His delusions about witches clouded his judgment

CHAPTER 15

The Secret Child

The next day, word spread that Ares and Eleanor had been killed by the King. The witches were outraged. No one knew that Amara had refused to help, and for now, it would remain a secret.

She felt guilty. At first, she thought she wanted Eleanor gone because she was jealous of her relationship with Henry. But now that Eleanor was dead, her conscience weighed heavily on her. She had never been jealous of anyone before. Of course, from time to time, she might have felt a twinge of jealousy toward other girls in the castle, especially those with mothers and no magic, but she had never been so jealous that she wished someone dead. Now she realised her impulses had gotten the better of her, and deep down, she wished she could go back in time. But she knew there was nothing she could do to bring them back.

She worried that Henry might never forgive her if he knew what she had done. Her conscience urged her to come clean to everyone, but she was too scared of how they would react. She decided to find Aiden; she needed to know what he thought of this whole situation.

When she found him, he was in a great hall, reading. Amara sat down, facing him.

"I have to tell you something."

He didn't look up from his book, and only a sound came from him: "Hmm?"

Amara took a deep breath. "It's my fault that Eleanor and Ares are dead."

He closed his book and stiffly looked at her. "What are you talking about? How is it your fault?"

"I…" She took a deep breath. "Henry came here to ask for help because my father held Eleanor in the dungeons. I refused and only let her father go. I didn't tell anyone. I didn't go with them."

Aiden's jaw tightened. He quickly stood up and started to pace. "You can't say anything to anyone about this, ever."

"Why? What would they do to me?" asked Amara.

"I don't know, but they will not understand."

He knelt in front of her. "Not a word. This stays between us. Promise me."

She smiled faintly. "I promise."

They ended the conversation before the rest of the witches arrived in the great hall for their meeting. Agnes wanted to speak to everyone about what had happened to Ares and Eleanor. She walked across the room in her long dark blue dress with bell sleeves. She turned to face them. "The King will pay for their lives with his own, and so will his nephew. I promise this to all of you."

"No, you can't do that," said Amara firmly.

"Amara, darling, it's the only way."
"I won't let you hurt Henry or my father."

"Well, you have no choice. Henry will die, and so will your father. They will pay for what they have done."

Amara wanted to argue further, but before she could say anything else, a large black window overlooking their front garden shattered. Glass flew all around them. Strong wind, darkness, and cold filled the room. Standing there, in the broken window, was a man. They couldn't see his face, only a dark, tall figure.

Agnes stepped in front of all the witches to confront whoever this was, with Amara and Aiden firmly behind her.

"Who are you? What do you want?" asked Agnes.

"Well, I want all of you dead, but for now I will settle for your attention." The man said in a deep voice.

"What are you talking about? Who are you?" Amara stepped forward.

The man chuckled and jumped down from the window. He began to walk towards Amara, but before he got too close, Aiden stepped in between them. "Too close, mate."

The man scoffed. "Ah, the strong, powerful, only son of Agnes."

Then he turned his attention to Agnes. He walked over to her and said, "Hello... mother."

Everyone in the room started to whisper, looking at each other with their eyes widening in disbelief.

"What are you talking about? I only have one son."

"Ah yes, yes, that's what you want everyone to believe, right?"

"Okay, I think you've said enough. You should leave," said Aiden.

The man chuckled and turned to face him. "I have not said nearly close to enough, brother."

"Mum, come on, what is he talking about?" asked Aiden.

Agnes looked at him, then at the man, and sat down. "Oliver?" She covered her mouth.

The man moved closer to her, bending over until he was just inches from her face. Aiden took a few steps to intervene, but Amara held his arm.

"Shall we tell them what really happened seventeen years ago? Hmm?" the man asked as he sniffed Agnes's hair.

He stood up, turned around, and looked at Aiden. "Seventeen years ago, when you, brother, were 1 year old, our beloved, caring, sweet, innocent mother wanted to come back here. She wanted to take what was hers. Well, at least she thought it was hers. Who knows why?"

He walked all around the room, turning suddenly. "Our father didn't just die on his own, you know. No, he died because someone..." he pointed at Agnes. "Played god."

His voice lowered. "You. You did it. You poisoned him. You poisoned our father, our grandmother, and our grandfather. Then you took him and left."

He looked into nothingness, then looked up, and then back down at Agnes. "You left me, though. I wasn't very important to you, was I?"

He told them that he was without food or water for two days. It was freezing outside when a wolf wandered into their cottage and saw him. In the wolf's eyes, he was just a small cub, so it took care of him.

Oliver suddenly shouted, frightening Agnes. "You left me there to die. What kind of mother does that?"

Everyone looked at Agnes in disbelief.

"Is this true?" Aiden stepped forward with tears in his eyes, gritting his teeth.

Agnes looked at Aiden and then at Oliver. "I have regretted it since; I wanted to come back for you, but I thought you didn't survive."

Oliver stood there, suddenly unbothered.

Agnes stood up to face him. "I didn't want to do it, but you didn't show any signs of magic." Her voice broke. "Aiden did. He showed his magical side when he was only six months old. I felt horrible, and I knew I had made a mistake, but I could not change the past."

Oliver laughed. "Well, you could always have come back for me. There's an idea. Maybe don't leave your little, vulnerable child on his own to die."

He smirked and said he wasn't there to play a happy family with them; he only came to tell them that a little bird had told him about King William trying to wipe them out from the Gulrose Kingdom, and he was here to help him. The only way he would get satisfaction was when all of those who had left and betrayed him were dead.

He walked up to Amara, with Aiden still shielding her. He looked her up and down and spoke.

"I have heard of your beauty and your power." He took a deep breath, glanced at Amara's lips, and continued, "I will be seeing you soon, love. I promise. We have a lot to do, you and me.

As he was about to leave, five large wolves leapt through the broken window and stood in front of him, growling.

Everyone stepped back. He gave Agnes one last eerie look. "This is my family now. Not you, and together we will end you."

Then he left the house through the same window he had shattered, with the wolves following right behind him.

Everyone was quiet, in disbelief. Aiden looked at his mother and then left the great hall, with Amara running after him. He was furious, walking towards the forest and mumbling to himself. "It can't be. She couldn't, she wouldn't."

Amara tried to calm him down, but it didn't do any good. He couldn't believe that his mother had killed his father and his grandparents and abandoned his brother. He let out a primal scream and fell to his knees. She wrapped her arms around him, trying to comfort him.

"We will get her for this, I promise you," she Amara.

Aiden sniffed. "I finished the replica. We are getting that pendant. Today."

Amara nodded, and together, hand in hand, they went back to the mansion to wait for the perfect opportunity to sneak into the basement and steal the pendant.

When they walked through the great hall, Agnes was there alone. She was sitting in an armchair, silent, with an empty look on her face. Amara and Aiden passed by to go to Aiden's room.

"Can I please explain?" asked Agnes in a desperate tone.

Aiden looked at her. "No, I don't want to listen to any more of your lies."

Agnes stood up quickly. "I was young, irresponsible, and hungry for revenge. I lost everything when Leopold fought against us. Please, you have to trust me. I regretted it every day."

Aiden stopped and turned his head halfway, not looking directly at his mother. "You regretted it so much that you never even thought about going back to see if he survived?"

Agnes stood there, lost for words. She knew what she had done all those years ago was evil and unforgivable.

Aiden continued, "No mother, this will not be an easy fix. We are all here to fight for our family, our coven, and for you. Well, I don't think people will want to risk their lives for you now."

He took one last look, grabbed Amara's hand, and walked off.

They went into his room, where Aiden showed her the emerald pendant replica. She was surprised, it looked the same, to the last detail.

"That's incredible, Aiden. When do we do this?"

"Tonight."

Agnes was still sitting in the great hall. She couldn't believe that everyone now knew what she had done. She thought her firstborn was long dead, and it wasn't ideal that he decided to come back now with everything that had been going on.

Yes, she had killed her husband, but she had no choice. He wouldn't let her and Aiden leave. Neither would his family. She had to eliminate them to be able to claim her birthright.

When Oliver arrived at his hiding spot with his wolves, he sat down in an armchair and laughed. He was very pleased with how it all went. This was his sole purpose for coming to Gulrose: to expose his mother to everyone and turn them all against her, especially Amara. He needed her for his plan.

"Did you see the look on Aiden's stupid face? Priceless," he said, looking at his wolves.

He got up and walked over to the mirror, looking at his reflection, his eyes wandering all around it.

"Soon, we will get everything we ever wanted. We will unite them all. We will get the girl—the most powerful being there is—and the woman who left me for dead will suffer. In her last moments, just before I kill her, she will know that I took Amara away from her."

One of the wolves came closer to him, looking up at him. Oliver listened and then rolled his eyes.

"Yes, we do need her. How many times do I have to tell you? She is the key to everything, and the best part is, she doesn't even know how important she is."

CHAPTER 16
The Unexpected Arrival

September 18, 1983,

"Tomorrow is my coronation. It was very strange to fight my own brother for the crown and I could never admit this to him, but I was terrified. William is a great swordsman, much better than I am. I still don't know how I beat him.

I feel a little bit guilty. I know he wanted this more than anything. I don't think he is ready, and I am not sure I am ready to rule the kingdom either. I know if father was here, he would much rather see William on the throne. They were the same. They wanted the same things. I am different and I am not so sure it's a good different. I am still being followed. I feel like I am losing my mind. There is a dark figure, everywhere I look there it is. There are dark thoughts in my mind whenever this person is around me. Like I am being bewitched."

Henry closed the diary, thinking about the last word: *bewitched*. Was this a clue that the murderer was indeed a witch? Maybe William was right, and the witches had killed his father. Perhaps they had intended to kill both of them, but for some reason, they had been unable to kill William.

It made sense. Without a king, it would be easy for the witches to take control of the kingdom. He closed the diary, got dressed, took Pearl and rode away.

He ventured deeper into the forest than he ever had before. His head felt like it was about to explode, overwhelmed by countless thoughts: Eleanor's and Ares' deaths, his father's death, the upcoming battle, and Amara.

Suddenly, he heard a loud growl. When he turned, he saw it—a manticore, staring directly at him. Before he could react, another growl echoed behind him, followed by another. He looked around and counted a total of five manticores. He was surrounded. The one that appeared to be the alpha stepped closer to Henry, so close that he could feel its breath on his face. Before he could do anything, the manticore sniffed him and began to walk in circles around him.

"Who are you? What do you want?" Henry asked, his voice steady despite the fear coursing through him.

The manticore didn't reply; instead, it took a few steps back and disappeared behind a tall tree. After a while a human emerged. Standing before him was a small dark-haired woman.

She smiled and said, "Hi, I'm Rebecca, and these are my friends."

Henry looked confused, but before he could ask any more questions, she spoke again. "I know your name is Henry, and I know who you are. We have been watching you for a while now."

"Me? Why?" Henry asked.

"Because we want you to join us, to join our pack and leave this place. There is no reason for you to fight this war. Join our pack and be free. This is not your fight."

"I didn't think there were any manticores left, except the royal family?"

"Yes, that's correct, well, technically," she replied.

There was a moment of silence. Henry's eyebrows raised, his eyes moving from left to right.

"Fine, no need for the suspense. Your father was my brother, my older brother, actually," said Rebecca.

He shook his head and stepped back. "Your brother? My father didn't have a sister."

Rebecca looked at him and raised her hand, gesturing for him to walk over to her. "Come, we have a lot to talk about."

Henry hesitated. For all he knew, this could be a trap. But why would it be? He had seen it with his own eyes. She was a shapeshifter, and so he followed her.

They walked for a while, her pack staying closely behind. She told Henry that she was two years younger than Peter and William. She loved them, and everything was great when they were younger, but she never got along with their father.

He always favoured the boys, especially from the moment they shapeshifted. Her transformation took a bit longer. Leopold didn't think she would ever change and thought less of her because of it. When Peter was killed, she ran away and never came back.

She was only 16 years old and all alone. Without anyone to take care of her, she didn't know how to survive on her own.

Eventually, she came across an older couple in the Glombort Kingdom, far away from there. They took pity on her, took her in, and she became part of their family.

The couple had four children—all boys—and for a while, she was happy. However, the mother, Anne, fell very ill and passed away two years later, leaving behind her husband, John, and their sons: Thomas, Patrick, Daniel, and Michael.

Rebecca took on the role of a homemaker, and soon the boys came to think of her as their sister. They were all years apart; the oldest brother, Thomas, was only two years younger than her. After another three years, John, the father, also succumbed to illness, leaving only the children behind.

Rebecca finally transformed, lived her life with the boys, and explored her strength as a manticore. They thrived together in their little cottage, and eventually, she changed them all. They formed their own pack, never to be parted. Then she heard about everything that had happened in the kingdom and of Henry's arrival.

She knew he wouldn't be safe with William and wanted to give him the chance to join her and her brothers. She believed that was what Peter would have wanted—Henry far away from this war.

Henry couldn't believe that William or anyone else had never told him about Rebecca.

"I am a royal manticore; I have to fight," said Henry.

"There are good and bad parts of being a manticore, and you're only concentrating on the bad ones. Not everything is about strength and power or about fighting a war. Sometimes it's just about finding peace within yourself."

After a while, the rest of the pack came to meet them, still in their animal forms. It was clear to Henry that they didn't trust him enough to approach as humans and preferred to remain in a form that would allow them to attack before he could even think about shifting. They introduced themselves to Henry through their thoughts, though they didn't seem particularly enthusiastic about being there.

He asked them to come back to the castle with him, confident that William would be pleased to see Rebecca again, especially with the cold night approaching. But Rebecca refused. She explained that William was the reason she had left all those years ago. When Peter died, she knew that William would become king and that the kingdom would suffer. She didn't want to witness everything that was about to unfold, so she had to disappear.

William was very much like their father—cruel, cunning, and manipulative. Peter, on the other hand, was like their mother—kind, caring, and empathetic. So, when Peter died, she knew this was no longer her home, and she needed to find a new one.

Henry appreciated the way she described his father but was less certain about her characterisation of William. He acknowledged that William could be impulsive and cruel at times, but he also cared about his people. Why else would he engage in a war?

He didn't know what to believe anymore. Everywhere he turned, people told him different things.

They talked for a little while longer until Henry left to return to the castle, promising Rebecca that he would come back the next day to meet with them. He wanted to learn more about his family and the past from her perspective.

When he came back to his room, he still wasn't completely convinced that she was telling the truth, so he went through more of his father's diaries to find out if he ever mentioned her. After many pages he finally found it.

June 10, 1977

"I caught father fighting with Becky again. He can't stand that she has not changed yet. He keeps comparing her to me and William. When he left, she

cried. I went to comfort her. She asked me to run away with her. Find a new life just the two of us, but I couldn't do it. This is our home, our kingdom, our people. They need all of us and even though father is being unreasonable, he can also be good. I begged her to stay, and she promised she would. I am hoping she will change soon.

I will speak to my father about this. He can't speak to her like this. Maybe it will change. Maybe he will understand and will stop being so hard on her. It's not her fault. Everyone is different and you can't push people. You have to give them time to find themselves.

William is more and more like him. Sometimes it terrifies me to think I have to deal with both of them. I don't know if I could do this without Becky."

September 12, 1977

"Me and Beccy went into the forest again. She tried to change but had no luck. It pains me to see her like this. I know she wants this more than anything. It's in our blood, it's who we are. I can't even imagine how she is feeling. She pretends to be strong, but I *know my sister. She is sensitive and always wants to please people. She feels like she is failing all of us. She doubts herself all the time and it keeps her from doing better.*

I wonder why she keeps failing. It took me a while to change as well but not this long. William had no problems with changing. Maybe the closer your heart is to the darkness the easier it is for you to change.

Father and William can both be a bit wicked, unlike me and Beccy.

Maybe that's the key to change. Darkness. Maybe I had some inside of me, that I didn't know of. Maybe I am also wicked, and Becky is the only one who is pure. She is still young. I am sure she will change soon."

Henry pondered this diary entry for a long time after reading it. Darkness might be the key to a manticore's transformation. What else was there to know about them? He yearned to uncover the truth about the curse that had created them, and that's when he thought of Eleanor. She would have known more about this, and if she didn't, she would at least know where to look.

He held his breath and pursed his lips, tears welling in his eyes as memories of her flooded his mind. Her perfect skin, her soft lips, her kind heart—she didn't deserve to die. She was pure, caring, and so young. And her father? He had only wanted to keep her safe. They had come here to help their kind, and instead, they had found death. Was this the fate that awaited everyone here in the end? Death and doom?

He got up and went to see William. Although he was still furious with him about Eleanor and Ares, he knew he had to talk to him. The hunters were to arrive the next day, and he needed to speak with him before that.

When he found him in the library, he simply walked in and sat down without saying a word. William looked away from his book at Henry, adjusted his glasses, and asked if he needed anything.

"First, I want to know how you could kill Eleanor and her father. They were innocent."

"There is nothing about them that is innocent, Henry. They just take and take, whatever and whoever they want," William replied calmly, setting his book on the table in front of him. He stood up, took a deep breath, and stretched his neck.

"They poisoned Amara with that nasty potion before she was even born to make her like them, my daughter. She was supposed to be only one thing: the mighty manticore. Instead, she is a filthy hybrid."

These words were like daggers to Henry's heart. How could her own father call her that?

"I know what they did. I will still fight beside you, but I need to know I can trust you," said Henry, walking closer to William.

"You know you can trust me. You know I tell you anything you ask me about."

"Really? You will? What about Rebecca? Why didn't you tell me about her?" asked Henry.

William looked shocked that Henry knew about her. He sat down, and without looking at Henry, he asked, "How do you know about her? Your father's diaries?"

"No, she told me herself. I met her today."

"What? You saw her? Is she okay?" William turned around, hope flickering in his eyes.

Henry shared a little bit about their conversation but didn't divulge too much. He still wasn't sure if he could trust William with everything. He told him how Rebecca had run away and where she ended up but kept quiet about her pack and their current whereabouts.

"Henry, listen to me. My sister wasn't as innocent as she's making herself out to be. Don't trust her that easily."

"What do you mean?"

"There was always something wrong with her. My father and I knew it, but for some reason, Peter didn't see it."

Henry pressed him about what exactly he thought was wrong with Rebecca, but William wouldn't elaborate. All he said was that she was dangerous when she was young, unpredictable, and he wouldn't be surprised if the old couple that found her didn't die of natural causes.

Henry didn't want to listen to this anymore and left the library. Just as he was about to step out, he heard William shouting behind him, "You will see I'm right! She can't be trusted. There was a darkness inside her that we could see slowly emerging, even though she tried to hide it well."

Henry fought the urge to turn back and ask more questions, but he knew he had to set everything aside until the battle was over. He didn't want to start another problem he would have to deal with.

CHAPTER 17

The Crossover

Aiden and Amara waited for everyone, especially Agnes, to go to bed. When the mansion was dark and silent, they slipped down to the basement with the replica in hand.

Amara hadn't realised just how eerie the basement would feel at night, with the whole mansion so quiet. They made their way through and finally stood before the small chest. They took out the blood and the fake pendant. Aiden began to chant a spell, letting a few drops of his mother's blood fall onto the chest.

"Öppna avslöja blodsbunden, öppna avslöja blodsbunden."

After a few seconds, they heard a click. They exchanged a look, and Amara nodded. Aiden opened the chest, and there it was—the real pendant. They could hardly believe they'd finally found it.

Aiden performed another spell to confirm it was indeed the real pendant, then they made the swap. Carefully, they resealed the chest with the same enchantment using the remainder of Agnes' blood, then left as quietly as they'd come.

When they reached Amara's room, she slipped the pendant around her neck, hiding it under her turtleneck. She knew the safest place to keep it was with her.

They were about to sit down when one of the witches burst into Amara's room, out of breath. He told them they needed to come downstairs immediately. When they arrived, the room was in chaos, with everyone talking over one another, arguing.

"What's going on?" Aiden shouted.

One of the witches told them they'd learned what the King had done: he'd secured help from the hunters, and they would be arriving soon. Another battle was near.

Amara was stunned. She'd thought the fighting was over, at least for now, but her father was coming for them once again. It felt as if this would never end until either he or Agnes was dead. She excused herself and left the mansion.

She ran into the woods, pushing herself until she couldn't run any farther. She dropped to her knees and screamed, releasing the rage that had built up inside her. A powerful wind whipped around her, as if an explosion had erupted. The force startled her; she hadn't realised she held this kind of power. Everything she'd been holding back burst out, like a bomb.

When she turned, she saw Henry standing there, staring at her.

What Henry saw frightened him. He took a few steps back, lifting his arms defensively. He'd seen Amara practising magic before, but this was different—so powerful that he could barely keep himself from stumbling as leaves whirled around him. Her eyes glowed an unnatural, piercing blue, and her hair floated with shimmering blue streaks through it.

"What are you doing?" he asked, his voice shaky.

Amara was breathing deeply, in and out. Then, with one final breath, her hair and eyes returned to normal.

Henry repeated his question, louder.

Amara looked at him, unsure. "I… I don't know." She paused for a moment and then asked, "Why are you here?"

"I just needed to be alone for a while. Didn't expect to run into anyone, especially you."

"Especially me? Nice," she said, standing up and brushing off her knees.

Henry rolled his eyes and rubbed his temple. "Look, I don't need any drama right now. I just want to be alone."

"Alone? You mean before the big battle?" She let out a small, bitter chuckle.

"I don't know what you're talking about," Henry replied, avoiding her gaze.

"Please don't lie to me. That was the one thing I actually liked about you—your honesty."

Henry looked down, shaking his head. "The one thing, hmm? I remember you liking much more than that."

He stepped closer, gazing intently into her eyes. "I never wanted this to happen. I thought… I thought we'd come here, and maybe we could be happy together. But then everything fell apart. We could never truly be together, and now… we're on opposite sides, fighting each other."

Amara moved closer; her expression hardened. "I know you and my father went looking for hunters. You found them, and now they're coming to help you destroy us."

"Amara, that's not what either your father or I want," he said, his voice edged with frustration.

"I won't let that happen, Henry. I won't let you harm anyone from my coven, no matter what I have to do,"

Before they could say another word, a low growl echoed from behind them. They turned to see a wolf—massive and black with piercing amber eyes. Henry's heart raced. It looked eerily like the wolf

Eleanor had once saved him from. Its gaze locked on them, menacing and unblinking.

Without hesitation, Henry stepped in front of Amara, shielding her with his own body. But then they both noticed more wolves emerging from the shadows, closing in, their eyes gleaming in the darkness.

They were surrounded.

"Amara, we need to shift."

"No, you need to shift; I can fight them with magic."

Henry closed his eyes, recalling the first time he'd shifted during the initial battle. He remembered the raw power he'd felt in that moment. When he opened his eyes, they were the colour of fire. He fell to his knees and shifted, still positioning himself protectively in front of Amara. He braced himself as one of the wolves lunged at him. The two collided, rolling and grappling, snarling and snapping at each other.

Meanwhile, the other wolves focused on Amara. She dodged their attacks with spells, countering each strike with precision. They fought for a while, until one of the wolves finally evaded her defences, pouncing on top of her. Henry caught sight of this, struggling to break free from the wolf he was battling, but his opponent held strong.

At last, Henry overpowered his attacker, turning quickly to help Amara—but she was gone. He searched frantically, his eyes darting through the shadows, only to realise that all the wolves had vanished as well.

Henry ran through the woods, desperately searching for any sign of Amara. When he heard nothing and saw no trace of her, he shifted back into human form and began shouting her name, his voice echoing into the dark. Panic surged through him as he grappled with the reality that she was gone. Why had the wolves taken her? What did they want with her?

Trying to gather his thoughts, he realised he needed help—and fast. William was an option, but deep down, he knew he'd be better off with someone who truly cared about Amara. Aiden was his best hope. He knew that Aiden loved Amara and would do anything to bring her back.

He hurried back to the castle, grabbed Pearl, and headed straight for the Black Mansion. He didn't bother knocking; there was no time for formalities. He burst through the doors, shouting Aiden's name.

"Alright, alright, I'm here," Aiden's voice called from the great hall. "You can stop yelling; it's annoying."

"Amara's been taken. We have to find her," Henry said, gasping for breath.

"What?" Aiden's face twisted in confusion and alarm. "What do you mean, taken? By whom?"

"I don't know," Henry replied. "We were in the woods, and a pack of wolves ambushed us. We fought them, but there were too many, and they took her. We have to go now."

"Alright, let's move. We'll get her back—whatever it takes," Aiden said firmly. He started to turn but then paused, narrowing his eyes at Henry. "Hold on—what do you mean you were in the woods? Why were you out there alone with her?"

"Now's not the time to get jealous. We have to find her," said Henry.

Aiden's lips tightened, his nostrils flaring. He knew he had to set his feelings aside and focus on finding Amara; the thought of anything happening to her was unbearable.

He told Henry he could perform a locator spell. Heading to her room, he grabbed her hairbrush and returned downstairs, arranging candles in a circle on the floor. He laid a map in the centre, placing the hairbrush on top of it. Turning to Henry, he said, "I'll need you to cut your hand so I can use your blood to help track her."

Henry raised an eyebrow. "You've got her hairbrush. Isn't that enough?"

"The more, the better. Your blood will sharpen the spell and point directly to where she is."

Henry grimaced. "Do I really have to cut myself? That's going to hurt."

Aiden rolled his eyes. "Oh, for heaven's sake. Here, I'll do it myself then." He grabbed Henry's hand and chuckled. "What, is the big, bad beast scared of a little cut?"

Henry sighed and held out his hand. Aiden made a quick incision, perhaps with a bit too much relish, and Henry winced, closing his eyes as a drop of blood fell onto the map. Aiden turned Henry's hand slightly to let more blood drop onto the paper, then began chanting.

"Ljus hitta Amara, Ljus hitta Amara."

The flames flared up, casting shadows that danced against the walls as the room's lights flickered. Slowly, the blood on the map began to stir and shift, though sluggishly at first. Aiden raised his voice, repeating the chant with renewed intensity until the blood finally started to move, tracing a path across the map. But instead of leading them to a single point, it formed a large, vague circle.

Henry squinted, frustration evident on his face. "What does this mean? I know the area, but it's massive—way too big to search on our own. Can't you make it more accurate?"

Aiden shook his head, frowning. "This shouldn't be happening. Something, or someone, is blocking me."

"Who could do that? And how?" Henry asked.

"It would have to be another witch," Aiden replied. Both men stood silent for a moment, processing the implications. They couldn't understand why any witch would take Amara—until Aiden's eyes widened as realisation struck him.

"It must be Oliver,"

"Oliver?" Henry looked at him, confused.

Aiden quickly explained what he'd discovered just the day before: the existence of Oliver, his long-lost brother, who he had never known about and who was now part of a wolf pack. The pieces began to fall into place, but they only raised more questions—and a chilling sense of urgency.

They decided to head into the vast area the blood had circled on the map, hoping they'd find Amara or, at the very least, some clue as to where she might be.

However, once they arrived, they were struck by just how massive and dense the area was.

Henry scanned the forest and then turned to Aiden. "I'll shapeshift—I might be able to track her scent."

Aiden raised an eyebrow. "You can do that?"

Henry shrugged, uncertain. "I don't know. I've never tried, but it's worth a shot."

Just as he was about to shift, a voice cut through the silence. "I know who you're looking for, but you're wasting your time. You're not going to find her. You might as well go home."

They turned sharply to see a figure emerging from the shadows. It was Oliver.

Aiden's expression darkened. "I was right. It *was* you. Why did you take her? What do you want with her?"

"It's not about what I want," Oliver said. "It's more about what I don't want: Amara being caught in the middle of a battle."

Henry's brow furrowed in confusion. "You… are you trying to protect her?"

Oliver smirked, his eyes glinting with a mix of cunning and ambition. "I have bigger plans for her, so for now, I need her alive."

Henry and Aiden asked more questions, but they didn't get any answer. Oliver jut looked at them and smiled. They tried to attack him, but it was very clear to them that he was much stronger than both. Physically and magically.

Henry looked at him, clenched his jaw and closed his eyes.

Aiden, sensing the tension, smiled at Oliver. "Now the fun can start."

Henry prepared to transform, but suddenly his body stopped, it refused. Aiden raised his hands, ready to cast another spell at Oliver. "What are you doing? Just do it! We stand a better chance if you're not yourself." He looked at Henry.

Henry glanced down at his trembling hands. "I can't. It's not working. Something's wrong.
It just… stopped."

Oliver chuckled and effortlessly hurled them both several meters away from where they stood. They landed hard on the ground, and as they struggled to regain their composure, Oliver's voice echoed. "Stay out of my way, or I will kill you both."

As he turned to leave, he paused and looked back over his shoulder. "See you later, brother." With that, he vanished into the shadows.

Aiden groaned, rubbing the dirt off his knees. "What was that? The one time I need you to come through, you fail me."

Henry sat up, resting his arms on his knees. "I don't know what happened. I felt this surge of energy, and then it just stopped. I think he did it. Somehow, he prevented my transformation."

Aiden looked at him, then walked over and reluctantly offered his hand. Henry took it, and Aiden helped him stand up.

"I wouldn't be surprised," Aiden said, shaking his head. "The magic I felt from my brother is powerful. He's strong—like Amara's level strong. It would be foolish of us to try to confront him now; on our own, we don't stand a chance."

"So, we just give up?" Henry asked, his frustration evident.

"No," Aiden replied firmly. "But for now, she's safe. If he wanted to hurt her, he would've let the wolves do it. Maybe it's for the best that she's not in the middle of the battle."

Henry nodded and took a deep breath. He didn't like this, but what Aiden was saying was right. At least she was safe for now, but it bothered him what Oliver had said about having other plans for her. He knew he would have to find out what those plans were and help her after the battle. They both agreed and went their separate ways.

Henry returned to the castle and told William what had happened, while Aiden did the same with Agnes.

When Oliver arrived at his hiding place, he went straight to see Amara. She wasn't in a cage or bound; she wasn't hurt. She was just sitting there, surrounded by wolves that guarded her.

Oliver ordered them all to leave, and they did. Amara looked at Oliver and asked, "How are you controlling them, and why can't I do magic?"

"You know, the first time I saw you, I recognised you immediately," he replied with an enigmatic smile.

Amara didn't like that he was avoiding her questions. Why would he do that? What was he hiding?

"You know, you are even more beautiful than I had heard. Powerful. It's very seductive," said Oliver, his tone flirtatious.

"HOW DO YOU CONTROL THE WOLVES AND WHAT DO YOU WANT WITH ME?" she shouted, her voice echoing in the silence.

Oliver smiled and sat down in front of her.

"Okay, no need to shout. I don't control them. I talk to them. They respect me because I respect them back; we are family. And you can't use magic because of that," he said, pointing at her right wrist.

She saw a silver bracelet that she didn't have on before.

"What is this?" she asked, eyeing the bracelet suspiciously.

"Another beautiful invention of our ancestors. It prevents you from using your magic, and only the person who put it on you can take it off."

"How do you speak to them?" Amara pressed.

Oliver looked down, smirked, and put his hand underneath his shirt. He pulled out a necklace. Amara recognised it; it looked exactly like the emerald pendant, only it was a mix of yellow and orange.

"What is that?" she asked, intrigued.

"This? This is the amber pendant. It allows you to speak to animals, to understand them."

Oliver explained everything to Amara about all the pendants and their powers. He told her he needed her to unite them all and to make him the pendant master.

She didn't understand any of this. The emerald pendant wasn't the only one. At that moment, she realised something and started to touch her chest frantically.

"Wait—my pendant! Where is it?" she exclaimed, panic rising in her voice.

Oliver held out the emerald pendant. "Now I have two; only three to go," he said with a satisfied smile.

"Why do you need me to unite them?"

Oliver stood up and began to pace around the room, the pendant glinting in his hand. "You might not be Agnes' child, but Agnes created your powers. She put a bit of her own power in the potion that she gave to Catherine all those years ago. That means you and Agnes are connected in a way you can't even begin to understand. I don't trust my mother, but for some reason, I think I can trust you."

"You have to let me go. My father will attack the witches soon, and I have to be there to help them fight," Amara insisted, desperation creeping into her voice.

"No. I need you alive," he replied firmly, stopping to face her.

"Nothing will happen to me. Please let me go, and I promise I will come back," Amara pleaded, her heart racing.

Oliver didn't trust her enough to let her go, but he saw an opportunity. If he allowed her to leave and she came back, it would mean she could be trusted.

So, he made the decision to let her go but he made it very clear that if she did not return after the battle, he would kill everyone she cared about.

"I will come back; I give you my word," Amara said firmly.

"Your word means nothing to me unless you prove it," he replied, crossing his arms.

"I will, I promise. Oh, and one last thing. Can I please have the emerald pendant back?"

Oliver chuckled. "Absolutely not. You know how hard they are to find?"

"I will come back with it. Please, I need it in case I have to use it against Agnes."

Oliver's brow furrowed in confusion. Why would she need it for Agnes? But then he had another idea. He would let her go and allow her to take the pendant with her, but only under two conditions. First, she had to return with it. Second, no matter what—whether she felt it was necessary or not—she had to use the pendant on Agnes and capture her power.

"Why?" she asked, a hint of suspicion in her voice.

"Because my mother is very, very powerful and I would like to use that power," he replied.

Amara agreed. She didn't have a choice. If she wanted to be near Aiden and Henry and make sure they were safe she had to agree with anything Oliver asked of her. "You have a deal," she said while holding up her wrist.

Oliver removed the bracelet and reminded her of the rules. She promised she would be back and then she teleported.

When she arrived at the mansion, she ran straight to Aiden's room. She burst in and startled him. He stood up fast and hugged her.

"Are you hurt?" He was frantically touching her face.

"No, he let me go."

Amara explained everything to Aiden and told him what she had to do. Aiden started to pace around the room, and then sat down massaging his forehead.

"Amara, I won't let you hurt my mum."

"No, not hurt. I just need to take her power."

"I am not going to let you do that either.

Please, I made a deal." Amara came closer to him.

"Well, I didn't make any." He looked up at her.

"Aiden, please. For me."

He took a deep breath and at the end, agreed. He and Amara talked for hours, coming up with a plan on how to catch Agnes off guard, so she wouldn't expect anything. They agreed that after the battle, would be their best chance.

CHAPTER 18

The Day Before

It was the morning before the battle. Henry woke up to a servant knocking on his door. She told him the King was looking for him and that he would be in the great hall waiting.

Henry thanked her and got dressed. When he went to the great hall to meet William, he saw a group of people talking to him. It was the hunters. They had arrived.

Henry approached and asked, "You were looking for me, Uncle?"

"Henry, yes, please come. We are planning our attack."

Elias waited for everyone to be seated and then told them his plan. A friend of his had informed him that the witches were now aware the hunters were there, so they didn't have the element of surprise anymore.

They would attack at dawn the following day, and they would fight at the location of the last battle.

They went through the plan in detail, discussing where the hunters would be stationed and where the King and his army would position themselves.

Then Elias snapped his fingers, and one of his hunters brought a large chest and placed it on a table. When he opened it, it was full of weapons they would typically use against witches.

There was a powder that would make them unconscious if you could get close enough. Of course, William already knew about this weapon; he had a few bottles himself. His soldiers had used it on Eleanor before they captured her.

Inside the chest were also crossbows, shackles, guns loaded with silver bullets, swords, arrows dipped in poison, and many more.

Lilian brought in another, much smaller chest. It was filled with small bottles of some liquid.

When Henry asked what they were, Lilian explained that the hunters had many weapons to fight against witches, but this one was probably the most important. It was an elixir that granted hunters their supernatural power, a power that could be compared to that of a manticore. Long before the hunters existed, there was a small village at the end of Mörkdimma. A child had been stolen from there by a witch, who later sacrificed it. The men of the village were outraged and wanted to kill the witch; however, she wasn't alone, and none of them stood a chance against her magic.

In this village lived a very old woman who was a sorceress. She never liked the term "witch," as she believed it was an evil name reserved for demons. She made a potion that would give the men a fighting chance against the witches.

After they drank it, they became fast, strong, and not as fragile as humans would be. They killed the witch and all of those who stood by her. When they returned to the village, they made a deal with the sorceress: she would make them potions so they could fight any witch that might come their way, and in return for her services, they would bring her whatever magical items she desired from the witches the hunters killed. This was over a hundred years ago, and the hunters had been hunting witches ever since. Before the sorceress died, they learned how to make the potion themselves and hired new hunters every year to expand their ranks.

However, it is very tricky to become a hunter. If you are not strong enough, the potion could turn you into a raging, uncontrollable, non-speaking, animal-like human, and the hunters would have to kill you.

"Did it ever happen?" Henry asked.

"Once," said Lilian. "We met a guy whom we thought had the potential to become a great hunter, but when he drank the potion..." She paused, trailing off.

"Let's say it wasn't pretty," Elias finished.

An uncomfortable silence fell over the room, and all the hunters lowered their heads.

William cleared his throat. "Well, I like this plan. I can already see a future without the witches, and it looks bright."

When the hunters left the great hall, Henry stayed behind, looking at all the weapons and wondering if this was going too far. His thoughts were interrupted by Catherine. She walked in and approached him.

"You know, you don't have to fight if you don't want to," she said to him.

"What kind of man would I be if I just sat here while they all fought? Besides, I need to make sure Amara is safe."

"Do you still love my daughter?"

"Yes, I do. But don't worry; I know we can't be together."

Catherine frowned. She knew Henry would be the perfect partner for her daughter. He loved her, cared for her, and would always protect her, but fate had a different plan. She stepped closer to him and revealed that she had been receiving letters from Amara. Every night, there was a letter on her bed from her. But in the last few days, Catherine had started to worry; Amara's letters had changed. They were darker and sounded less and less like Amara.

Henry understood her concerns. He too believed that since Amara had been spending more and more time with Aiden, her old personality had faded, giving way to a new, darker version of herself. She had become powerful and scary, and he couldn't shake the feeling that the change was a threat to everyone around her.

They didn't know what Amara would do during the battle. Would she protect everyone, as she had done in the first one? Or would she turn against them and kill? She had the power to do either.

Catherine also shared another concern with Henry. When she had drunk the potion eighteen years ago, she hadn't fully understood its power. After Amara was born and Catherine left for London to find the only weapon that could save them from Agnes, she had conducted extensive research about the potion. Theodore had helped her gather the information she needed.

Agnes had created the potion so that the Queen could become pregnant and bear a child with magical powers. However, what they didn't know was that Agnes had infused a large amount of her own power into it, which meant that a great deal of the darkness that resided within Agnes was also inside Amara. While Amara had never acted on it before, Catherine was now worried that the more time she spent with Agnes and Aiden, the more she would change and embrace that darkness. After that, they would never be able to bring her back.

Henry assured the Queen that they would win the battle and retrieve Amara before it was too late. Catherine smiled, feeling grateful to have Henry on her side. He was kind and strong, just like his father.

After they finished their conversation, Henry ventured into the woods to meet Rebecca and her pack. He knew he needed to convince them to join the fight.

When he arrived at the place they had agreed to meet, no one was around. He couldn't hear a sound. He sat down, taking in the beautiful nature around him, when suddenly Rebecca appeared, alone.

"Where are the others?" Henry asked.

"They only came the first time because I didn't know if I could trust you," she replied.

Henry looked at her with a smile on his face. "We need you to fight with us tomorrow. Please."

"I'm sorry, Henry, but this is not our fight."

Henry didn't understand. It was their fight too. This was a battle between witches and humans, but Rebecca felt differently. This conflict had begun hundreds of years ago. Each king had harboured a hatred for witches without reason and sought to rid the kingdom of them. Rebecca didn't want to give in to the madness that each ruler of this kingdom seemed to have.

"I understand, but the battle is happening anyway. Amara and I will be there, and we will fight. Can you do this for us, for your family?" he asked.

Rebecca sighed deeply. She didn't want her nephew and niece to be in danger; she also couldn't believe they were fighting against each other.

Henry didn't give up. He told her everything he and Amara had gone through and how Amara had embraced her darkness. If they didn't save her, she would succumb to it completely, then it would be too late.

"Oh Henry. I don't know. I can't risk the lives of my pack for my mad brother's desires, but I do care for both you and Amara."

In the end, she agreed to take this back to her pack and leave the decision to them. She told Henry to meet her again that evening and she would let him know what they had decided.

Henry went back to the castle, hoping that deep down, the pack would know that fighting beside them was the right decision and that their answer would be yes.

When he arrived back, he saw all the hunters training, Lilian included. She wore black trousers and a black long-sleeve shirt, her dark hair in a French braid. Henry watched her for a bit, and for the first time, he was enjoying the view. Her shining blue eyes and beautiful smile captivated him. She noticed his gaze and stopped fighting.

"Are you just going to stare, or are you going to train? The battle is tomorrow, you know," she shouted from a distance, a teasing smile playing on her lips.

Henry chuckled and picked up a sword lying nearby. He approached her, ready to challenge her, but he quickly realised that Lilian was not the type of person to underestimate in a fight. She was quick on her feet and strong. Before he knew it, he found himself on the ground with a sword pointed under his chin, looking up at her with a mix of surprise and admiration.

"I might have to stay close to you during the battle," he chuckled, still trying to catch his breath.

"That's probably not the best idea; I might just get distracted," she replied, a teasing smile on her face.

He stood up and retrieved his sword, taking a moment to compose himself. Lilian took a few steps back, ready for his next move. Henry charged at her, lifting his sword and slashing towards her. She met his strike with hers, their faces inches apart, the tension clearly visible between them.

With a grin, she lifted her right leg and kicked him in the stomach. He flew a few meters away, landing on his back, coughing and laughing at the same time.

Lilian approached him, extending her right hand to help him up. "You really need to work on your technique," she said playfully.

"Yeah, yeah. I think I'm getting the hang of it," he replied, accepting her hand and rising to his feet. He felt a surge of adrenaline and determination. "Let's go again, but this time, I'll try to stay on my feet."

Lilian nodded, stepping back into her fighting stance. "Good luck with that!"

They resumed sparring, and with each exchange, Henry found himself becoming more attuned to her movements, pushing his limits while enjoying the challenge. Amidst the clash of swords and their laughter, he felt a fleeting moment of normalcy before the storm of battle arrived. The connection between them grew stronger.

"Wow," Henry gasped at her.

"Again?" she asked.

In the end, he agreed to a rematch—anything to spend a little more time with her.

They trained for a little while longer before everyone went back to their chambers. Henry returned to the forest, hoping to see Rebecca there and to get an answer to his question. He waited for a while, and when she showed up, the pack was there with her. They were all in their human form. All the boys looked very similar. Tall, dirty blond hair and green eyes, muscles Henry could only dream of.

"We have come to a decision," said Rebecca while Henry eagerly waited, preparing for potential disappointment.

His heart was beating fast, as if it were about to jump out of his chest.

"This one time only, we will join you. We will fight side by side with you," she said.

Henry was ecstatic, but before he could say anything, Rebecca spoke again. "But we have one condition."

"Yes? What is it?" he asked.

She looked him up and down. "After the battle is done and we win, you will come with us. You will join our pack, and so will Amara. You have to find a new life for a while—somewhere where you both can be yourselves."

Henry was surprised by this request, but he knew that right now he had to agree to anything they asked of him, so he did.

They said their goodbyes, and he went back to the castle, feeling victorious.

He couldn't sleep that night. He knew tomorrow's battle would be more brutal than the first one, but he was quite confident that with the hunters and with Rebecca and her pack on their side, they would win.

In the meantime, Oliver made his way to the castle. He asked to be seen by the King. The guards escorted him inside, where he patiently waited.

When William finally showed up, he didn't know who Oliver was, and he didn't really want to waste his time with the battle happening the next day.

He thought he would just listen to what this man wanted to say and send him on his way, but when Oliver told him who he was, William knew there was a long conversation ahead of them. He took Oliver into the library and closed the door behind them.

Oliver explained what had happened to him when he was younger, how Agnes had abandoned him, and that he wanted to take revenge on her.

William wasn't that sure at the start. He was fighting against witches and didn't want to have one on his side, but he realised that with Oliver and his wolves, alongside the hunters, manticores, and his soldiers, the witches didn't stand a chance. Just as they were talking, Henry walked in. He stopped at the door and looked at both.

"Henry, my boy. Come. We gain another ally," said William.

Henry made his way to sit down beside William, who told him everything he had just heard. Henry looked Oliver up and down.

"Uncle, can I speak to you alone?" asked Henry.

"Later, Henry. We have a guest now. We wouldn't want to be rude, would we?"

Oliver continued to tell them how much he despised his mother and how much he wanted to make her suffer. He explained what had happened with Amara, assuring them that she was safe and that he would never hurt her. He also mentioned the deal they had made.

"I will offer you another thing," said Oliver.

"And what is that?" asked William.

"I know you want Amara back. She is quite fond of my brother, isn't she?"

This was like a knife to Henry's heart. His expression changed immediately. Whenever he felt like he was getting over her, hearing someone mention her and Aiden together reminded him that he wasn't.

"What if I tell you that I can ensure my brother does not survive this battle? Amara will not be able to blame either of you for his death, and without him, I am sure she will return to you willingly."

William smiled, and the look on his face sent chills down Henry's spine.

"You have yourself a deal, boy," said William.

They shook hands, and Oliver stood up to leave. As he passed Henry, who was sitting in an armchair, he stopped beside him, leaned down, and whispered, "Now the real fun is about to start," then he left.

Henry stood up quickly and said, "Uncle, this doesn't feel right. He kidnapped Amara. He's willing to kill his brother and destroy his mother? What type of person does that?"

"I don't care about any of this. I want them gone. He can do whatever he wants to them as long as he's on our side."

That was the problem, though. Henry thought that if Oliver was willing to do all of this, who knew what he might do to them afterward? But there was no convincing William; he had decided Oliver would be fighting alongside them in the battle.

"Well, I have some good news myself," said Henry.

William listened eagerly. Henry told him that he had secured Rebecca's support and that she and her pack would also fight with them. William's expression changed from a smile to a frown. He hadn't seen his sister in eighteen years. She had run away and never returned. He thought all this time that she was most likely dead. She hadn't even had the courtesy to come back and speak to him, but in the end, Henry convinced William that this was a good thing and that after the battle, they might be able to mend things between them.

"You have lost one sibling. Make sure you don't lose the other," said Henry before he left.

CHAPTER 19

The Day Of

Everyone woke up early and got ready for the fight. Larrus and his tribe arrived at the Black Mansion, where he and Agnes explained the plan for the battle to all who were fighting.

Larrus and Agnes were confident they could win this battle and finally be free of William's reign of terror. However, this time they knew they had to kill him if they didn't want to face him again in the future. They understood that if he lived, this conflict would never end.

They packed up their weapons and made their way to the battlefield. At the same time, the King and his army were also heading to confront them. When both sides arrived, William and Agnes did not speak to each other as they had before the first battle.

Henry was searching for Amara in the crowd of witches, and when he spotted her, he saw that she was standing hand in hand with Aiden. Her hair was pulled up, and she was dressed in black trousers, a dark blue long-sleeved shirt, and a purple cape. Aiden shot Henry a smug look and pulled Amara closer to him. In that moment, Henry felt as if his eyes could spit fire.

William gave the order, and his soldiers began to advance. Agnes and Larrus smiled; there were only a handful of them, and they thought this would be an easy win. But before they could even move, they suddenly spotted another army approaching. Five manticores charged at the front, followed by wolves with Oliver in command, riding one of them. Beside them were the hunters, all rushing toward Agnes. The witches took a step back, fear etched on their faces.

"Stay firm!" shouted Larrus.

William's side continued moving closer to the witches. Larrus drew his sword and screamed, "CHARGE!"

All the witches and centaurs rushed toward the King's large army. Henry and William changed mid run, now ahead of all their soldiers, almost catching up to the wolves and Rebecca's pack.

When the two sides collided in the middle, Henry found himself facing one of the centaurs, who reared up and was about to stamp on him. Luckily for Henry, he was quick. He dodged the attack, leaped onto the centaur's back, and bit its neck. The centaur screamed in agony, causing Larrus to turn to see what had happened. When he saw a manticore attacking one of his own, he quickly killed the soldier he was occupied with and ran toward Henry to help his friend.

He drew his sword and was only a few inches away from Henry. He raised his weapon, ready to kill, but before he could do anything, another manticore charged at him and bit him in the face. Larrus fell to the ground while the manticore finished him off. It was Rebecca who had just saved Henry's life.

Agnes heard his screams. She turned around and saw his life being taken. A single tear slid down her cheek. He was dead. She bent forward and screamed so loudly that Aiden and Amara stopped fighting and looked in her direction. Agnes ran to Larrus and collapsed beside his body. His eyes were wide open, but he wasn't breathing. She touched his face lightly and then gently closed his eyes while tears continued to stream down her face. Her expression suddenly shifted from sorrow to fury. She stood up and glared in the direction of Henry and Rebecca; of course, she didn't know it was them, but she didn't care.

She cast a curse and sent a bright red light in their direction, but before it could hit them, it stopped right in front of their faces. When they turned, they saw Oliver; he had stopped the curse and redirected it towards another group of witches, hitting one of them, killing her instantly.

Agnes couldn't believe that her own son had just killed one of their own. He winked at her, then suddenly vanished.

William came face to face with Amara. She recognised him immediately; every manticore was a bit different from one another. William's form was dark, almost black, with a white streak running down his side. And of course, they could communicate through their thoughts. They locked eyes for a moment, then William turned and walked away. This didn't make Amara sad; it filled her with anger, a deep, seething rage.

Her own father didn't care enough about her, even during a deadly battle. She moved forward and struck one of the hunters with a spell. The hunter fell in agony, with another strike, she bound his hands and feet together. He tried to escape, but he had no chance of breaking free. Aiden came closer to the hunter, looked down at him, lifted his sword, and stabbed him in the heart, killing him instantly.

He smiled, looked at the dead body, and twisted the sword inside him before pulling it out. He was still standing above the hunter when someone kicked him in the chest with such force that he fell to the ground. He quickly stood up to face whoever had attacked him. Standing in front of him was Lilian. She swung her sword behind her back, her lips pressed together, and said, "You shouldn't have done that."

Then she attacked him. He kept dodging her attempts to cut him with spells, but she was too fast for him. They fought each other for a few seconds before she stabbed him in the stomach, causing

Aiden to fall to the ground. As he knelt there, bleeding, she came closer, grabbed his hair, and kicked him in the face with her knee. Then she left to fight others. Aiden lay on the ground, bleeding out quickly, pressing on his wound and coughing up blood.

Amara ran to Aiden and slid on the ground next to his body. "Oh my god, what do I do? Tell me what to do!" But Aiden couldn't speak; blood was pouring out of his mouth.

She knew she didn't have much time to save him. She teleported them back into the Black Mansion. As he lay on the couch, she performed a healing spell.

"Laka inuti," she said, then she looked at him and touched his hair over and over again. "This should hold you for now, but I have to go back. I have to finish what we started," she cried.

When she reappeared on the battlefield, she had a clear target: Lilian. She finally found her in the large crowd of people. Lilian was slashing one witch after another when Amara, while walking, lifted her hand

and, with one movement, levitated Lilian into the air, making her drop her sword. From the corner of her eye, Amara could see another hunter running at her. She held Lilian in the air with one hand while she choked the hunter to death with the other.

Now standing below her, Amara prepared to bring her down fast, smashing her into the ground to kill her. But before she could do that, Henry lunged at her, knocking her down. Lilian was now falling, and just before she could hit the ground, Oliver slowed her descent.

Amara was now standing face to face with Henry, but neither one of them wanted to attack. Henry would never hurt her; he just wanted to save Lilian. Amara got frustrated and picked another target. So did Henry.

The battle was slowly coming to an end; the witches were obviously losing, with only a few of them and a handful of centaurs still alive.

Amara knew it was now or never. She sneaked up behind Agnes and took out the emerald pendant. As Agnes fought, she suddenly felt something strange inside her. She didn't know what was happening, and when she turned, she saw Amara approaching with the pendant raised and glowing. She was chanting the absorption spell.

"Strom in innesluta, strom in innesluta."

Agnes tried to fight it, but there was nothing she could do. A shiny green light emanated from her chest and into the pendant. She fell to her knees, attempting to cast spells, but nothing worked.

"Why? Why did you take my power?"

"Because someone like you should never have had this much power in the first place." Then Amara waved her hand and sent Agnes into a cell that was waiting in Oliver's cabin in the woods.

She quickly put the pendant back around her neck and hid it under her shirt, making sure no one saw what she had just done. She looked around and saw the witches struggling to keep up the fight. William's army was too strong. They had many powerful allies on their side, and she knew the rest would be slaughtered. She closed her eyes and sent a mental message to all the witches and centaurs on the field.

"Witches and Centaurs, we will not win this fight today. Many of us have already died. Let's retreat and find another way for our coven to be free."

Then she opened her eyes and saw all those on her side nodding in agreement. All the witches disappeared from the battlefield, retreating. The King's army celebrated their victory.

When Oliver and his wolves arrived at their cabin, he was pleased to see Agnes in the cage without her powers.

"Hello, mother."

"Why am I here, Oliver?"

Oliver smiled. "Well, I did tell you I would make sure you suffered. I am going to get something to eat and then I need a long sleep. We will start the unpleasantness tomorrow."

Agnes frantically looked around, trying to figure out how to escape, but it was in vain. The cell was very well built, and she didn't have her powers. Unless someone came to save her, she would be stuck there.

Her back slid against the wall as she sat on the cold ground, rocking back and forth. She couldn't believe Larrus was dead and that she was here. Amara had betrayed her, and her own son had imprisoned her. She screamed out of frustration.

When Amara arrived at the Black Mansion, she ran straight to Aiden. She was about to tell him how she had succeeded in absorbing Agnes' power, but when she finally saw him, she froze. Aiden wasn't moving, and he was pale—unnaturally pale. She ran to him and touched his hand, calling his name. His hand was cold. She shook him before realising what had happened. He was dead.

She didn't understand. She had put a healing spell on him; it was supposed to help with his wound and allow her to treat him after the battle. What had she done wrong?

Amara cried and screamed his name, sobbing as she stroked his hair. A few witches that were left ran over to see what was happening, and when they saw

Aiden dead, they tried to comfort Amara. But she struggled against them and grabbed the black book of spells.

"I don't understand; I did it properly. I did it properly," she kept repeating.

The witches were confused. What had she done properly?

"He can't be dead. He just can't. I can't lose him." She kept going through the book, trying to find a spell to help him. The witches told her there was no spell that could bring him back, but she knew that was a lie. She knew there was one; she just had to find it.

"Amara, you cannot use this spell. It takes hold of your soul, and you will never be the same. You will succumb to the darkness, and there is no coming back from it. The devil himself will have a hold on you," said one of the witches.

But Amara didn't care; she would do anything to bring Aiden back. After moments of searching, she finally found it. She ordered the witches to carry

Aiden into the middle of the room and lay him on the floor. When they reluctantly did, she placed candles all around him and got ready to perform the spell, even though the witches begged her not to do it.

She wiped away her tears and started to chant.

"Dakr makt jag kallar dig."

The deeper she went into the enchantment, the stronger she felt. She looked down at her hands, and black veins started to appear; they travelled all the way up her arms and her neck. When they reached her face, she gasped, mouth open, eyes closed. When she opened her eyes again, they were completely black—not just her pupils but the entire surface of her eyes. She kept chanting; it was like she was in some kind of trance. Suddenly, Aiden woke up. It looked like his soul had jumped back into his body. When he did, Amara stopped, looking normal again, but feeling different. She fell next to Aiden, sobbing. "You're back; it worked. You're here."

Aiden looked out of place, confused. "What happened?"

"Well, you got injured, and I thought you would be fine with a healing spell, but when I came back, you were gone."

"Gone? You mean dead? How am I back?" He paused before saying, "Amara, what have you done?"

CHAPTER 20

The Day After

Everyone in the castle celebrated. They had finally defeated their enemy.

They all believed the remainder of those who survived would now scatter all over Mörkdimma, and they would not have to face them ever again.

Henry went to see William. The battle the day before had made him realise that maybe it was not such a bad idea to go away with Rebecca and her pack for a while. He could explore who he really was and run free. He needed some time away from all of the "witches versus humans" obsession that William had, but when he found him and told him his plan to leave for a while, William wasn't happy.

He wanted Henry to stay, and he actually wanted his sister to stay as well. He said he would welcome her and her pack, but what Henry didn't know was that there was a more sinister reason behind this, and

William's intentions were not as honourable as he made them out to be. Henry thanked William and told him he would talk to Rebecca about this, but for now, he needed to go with them, at least for a while.

"Henry, you can't just leave. What about Amara? We need to bring her home now," said William.

"I think she and I need some time away from each other. A lot has happened, and I am not sure we will ever be the same as we were before," said Henry as he was leaving the library.

He went straight to Catherine's chambers and knocked on her door. When he went inside, he saw her sitting at her window, looking out at the castle's gardens. When she saw it was him who had paid her a visit, she smiled, but there was something wrong with her look. She appeared tired—no, not tired; exhausted.

"Hello, Henry," she said quietly.

"Is everything alright?"

"Come, come, sit with me."

She took Henry's hand in hers and looked into his eyes. She told him she didn't want to say anything before the battle, but she didn't have time to keep this to herself anymore.

She was sick. She had been ill for about a year now, and she didn't have much time left. She begged Henry to bring Amara back to her so she could say her goodbyes.

Henry's eyes filled with tears. Catherine had become like a second mother to him in the short time he had known her. He had sent his mother away to keep her safe, and now he was about to lose Catherine too.

They sat together for a bit while Catherine told him stories about her life in London. She liked it there. The only thing that was missing, of course, was Amara, but she enjoyed her job in the little boutique. She appreciated the fact that no one had to be scared of magic. It was the simple life that she missed. She felt guilty admitting this, but sometimes she wished that when Amara had found her, they had stayed in London instead of coming back to Gulrose.

Henry understood why she felt that way, but he also knew that even though they had to fight, he loved it here. This was their home, and they had to protect it from those who wanted to destroy it.

He promised he would speak to Amara, hugged Catherine, and left. He didn't tell her about his plan to leave with Rebecca; he knew she had more than enough to deal with.

He went straight to the stables and grabbed Pearl. He raced to the Black Mansion to convince Amara to go to the castle with him and speak to her mother. When he arrived, he saw some witches leaving. He knocked on the door and waited. A young witch he recognised from the battlefield opened the door. Henry explained why he was there, and the girl invited him in. He sat down in a hall and waited. Soon he heard footsteps. He expected it to be Amara, but when he turned, he saw Aiden. Henry's face went white.

"Aiden? I saw you being wounded in the battle. How did you survive that?"

"I didn't. Not really." Aiden sighed and sat in front of Henry.

He told him that he had died, and Amara had brought him back to life with a dark spell that no one should ever use.

"It should have killed her, but it didn't," he said.

He explained that it had changed her. Her soul was already darkened from the things she had done and from the spells she had used, but this had finished her soul off. They had argued, and she had left to give the pendant to Oliver, and he hadn't seen her since.

Henry couldn't believe it. He needed to find her and tell her about her mother, but neither he nor Aiden knew where Oliver was staying, and they realised his place would be cloaked, so Aiden would not be able to find out where they were.

They did not like each other; they were rivals, but even Aiden recognised that Henry really needed to speak to her, so he offered to help him. He said he could send her a note wherever she was, even without knowing the exact spot. Henry wrote a note on a piece of paper, and Aiden crumpled it in his hand. He held it tightly, closed his eyes, and started to chant. He opened his hand, the paper caught fire and disappeared.

"Done," said Aiden.

"Thank you," said Henry. He then stood up, and as he was walking away to leave the mansion, Aiden shouted after him.

"Hey, we don't like each other, and I hope I won't have to see you again, but if she comes to see you, please tell her to come back home," said Aiden.

"This is not her home, Aiden. Her home is with me and her kind."

Henry went straight to where Rebecca and her pack were staying. They were all ready to leave; only waiting for him. When he arrived without any bags, Rebecca

frowned. "Why aren't you ready to leave?"

Henry looked at her and explained the situation. He said he wanted to go with them, but he couldn't leave Catherine. He begged Rebecca and the boys to stay until Catherine passed so she wouldn't have to do this alone. After a little consideration, they agreed. They promised to stay and wait for Henry, but as soon as Catherine was gone, they would leave without any further delay. What they didn't know was that everyone would come to regret this decision.

Henry went back to the castle and told William everything that had happened. William wore a small smile, but it wasn't because he cared for his sister and wanted to spend time with her; it was because it played perfectly into his plans. After their conversation, Henry went to see Catherine to tell her everything. She was happy that he decided to stay with her, but she felt guilty for stopping him from truly understanding who he was and from spending time with his aunt.

Henry smiled. "I can still do that, but right now you need me here, and I want to be here with you."

Catherine had always known of his kindness, and now more than ever, she needed it.

As they sat there talking, a cold breeze suddenly filled the room, then they heard a whooshing sound behind them. When they turned, they saw a figure standing there. It was Amara. They almost didn't recognise her. She was dressed in a dark blue hooded dress, with black gloves, and she proudly wore the emerald pendant around her neck.

"Hello," she said simply.

"Amara," said Catherine. She got up and went to hug her daughter, but when she did, Amara did not hug her back.

"Henry, could you leave us?" asked Amara.

"Oh, yes, of course. But please, can I talk to you before you disappear again?"

"I don't have much time, sorry."

"Please, it will only take a minute, and it's important," said Henry, hoping she would agree.

And she did. She promised she would find him, and they would talk. When he left, Amara sat down.

Her mother looked her up and down, pointing out that she almost didn't recognise her own daughter but made sure to tell her she looked beautiful.

Amara told her that this had always been her; she just needed to explore her own power and embrace it. Catherine informed her about her illness and begged Amara to stay with her because she didn't have much time left. To her surprise, Amara refused. She still loved her mother somewhere deep down, but this new Amara had her own path now, and she couldn't turn back. Catherine was heartbroken. Her own daughter did not want to spend her last moments with her. Tears began to fill her eyes as she felt she had failed her daughter, unable to protect her from evil, from Agnes.

Amara kissed her mother on the forehead and said, "Goodbye, Mother," before she disappeared.

Catherine kept screaming her name over and over. Henry was waiting outside, and when he heard her screams, he rushed inside to find Catherine falling into his arms. She told him everything that had happened. Henry couldn't understand why Amara would just leave her dying mother. He didn't even care that she hadn't come to speak to him; leaving Catherine in this state filled him with disgust and rage.

When Amara arrived at the cottage she was staying at with Oliver, she was visibly distressed, and Oliver could see it.

He asked her, "What happened? Where did you go?"

"I went to see my mother," she replied.

"You know I don't want you to get distracted from our goal."

"I know. She is dying, so she won't be a distraction for very long," Amara said.

Oliver liked her answer. She had finally crossed the dark path he had always wanted her to.

"Why me? Why did you choose me?" she asked.

"You are very important, very powerful. I've known it for a long time. You and I, together, will be indestructible. Together, we can rule wherever we want and take whatever we desire."

Amara asked him what he meant by "a long time." Oliver explained that when his mother left him as a toddler, he vowed he would never feel powerless or in need of love again. When he heard about Amara's birth and the circumstances surrounding it, he realised she would possess an unbelievable amount of power. He knew he had to meet her but had to wait for the right moment—when she would finally explore her dark side.

"You mean evil?" she asked.

"I don't believe in good or evil, Amara. No one is solely one or the other. I prefer to call it dark and light power. You just have to be brave enough to explore both."

They went into the basement, where Agnes was being kept. When they opened the door, Agnes flinched. She had been there for days, barely receiving any food or water.

"Hello, mother," said Oliver.

"Amara, please, help me," she whimpered.

"She isn't going to. She knows where her loyalty lies," Oliver replied.

Amara continued to watch Agnes with an eerie look. She stepped closer and said, "You know I despise you. You are an embarrassment. You shouldn't have any power. You don't deserve it."

Agnes pleaded with her, trying to convince her to help, but Amara was firm.

"I suppose I should thank you, though. You made me who I am. Without you, I wouldn't have this power. So, thank you; at least you did something right."

Agnes asked them what they planned to do with her. Oliver laughed and told her they wouldn't kill her. They needed her, and as soon as she revealed where the rest of the pendants were and how to unite them, they would release her.

Agnes didn't want to tell them. She knew she wasn't the purest witch and had made many mistakes in her life, but whoever united the pendants would possess a power so dominant that no one would ever be able to defeat them.

"I already told you. I don't know," she demanded.

"And I already told you, I know you're lying," said Oliver, expressing his disappointment. "Well, you're giving me no other choice, mother." He looked at Amara and nodded.

They both grabbed Agnes and tied her to a chair. She struggled, but she was too weak to stand a chance against them.

Amara stood in front of her, and Agnes waited for what was coming. Without saying a word, Agnes suddenly couldn't breathe. She was choking, her eyes wide with panic as she looked at Amara.

"You see, you limited Amara's powers a lot. She doesn't need enchantments to be spoken aloud for simple spells. She is so powerful that just the thought of you choking can make it happen," said Oliver.

Agnes was without air for a while; she began to turn blue. Just before she could pass out, Amara stopped.

"Where are the rest of the pendants, mother?" asked Oliver.

Agnes did not say a word. Amara closed her eyes and stretched her neck. Suddenly, Agnes felt very strange; she began to see things that weren't there. She was standing on top of a cliff. She looked down and saw the ground below. The cliff was so high that if she fell, it would mean instant death. Suddenly, she heard footsteps behind her, and before she could turn, someone pushed her. Now she was falling to her death. Agnes screamed, and just as she was about to hit the ground, she was back in the chair, bound. She was breathing heavily, looking around, her hands shaking. Amara had made her experience this many times, forcing Agnes to feel as though she was falling to her death over and over again.

Oliver sat there, enjoying the show. "As you can tell, she is also very good at visual projection."

"Please, no more," Agnes cried.

Oliver looked at Amara. "Shall we try something else?"

Amara smiled and turned back to Agnes, who now felt a burning sensation in her hands. When she looked down, her hands were turning red, as if they were on fire from the inside. It was the most excruciating pain she had ever experienced. She screamed so loud that she could barely hear what Amara said next.

"Tell us where they are and how to unite them, and I will stop."

Agnes fell quiet for a moment as Amara closed her eyes again.

"No, no more, please. I will tell you. I will tell you." Agnes let out a heavy breath. She felt defeated; the pain was overwhelming.

She relented and told them what they already knew: they possessed two of the pendants. The emerald pendant hung around Amara's neck, while the amber one rested around Oliver's. The remaining three were scattered around the world. The lilac pendant was hidden in Dodblomma, protected by an ancient and powerful original witch hunter. The maroon pendant was in Glombort, guarded by a pack of manticores. And the last one, the navy pendant, was in a place that should never be entered—Skadlig. It was claimed by the foulest creatures known to man:

the draugar. Their leader wielded the pendant against his enemies.

"Draugar? But they can't be real, can they?" Amara asked, a hint of disbelief in her voice.

"You've heard of them?" Oliver asked, his brows furrowing.

Amara narrowed her eyes at him. "Yes, Theodore used to tell me terrifying stories about them. But I thought they were just myths."

Agnes chuckled. "Oh, they are very real."

"And how do we unite the pendants?" Oliver asked.

Agnes explained that only someone from their bloodline could perform the union. But the spell came with a grave warning: it would claim the caster's life if they were not strong enough.

Oliver pointed out that Amara counted as part of their family because her power was created by Agnes.

Agnes told them they would find the spell in the basement of the Black Mansion. It was hidden in a little black chest set into the walls of the basement.

Her ancestors wanted to make sure no one would ever be able to read it, so they put an enchantment on it. You could only read it fully when you had all the pendants.

Amara and Oliver smiled, put Agnes back in her cell, and left.

Agnes felt defeated. She didn't want to tell them all of this, but she had to. She could not bear the pain. She thought there was not much harm in telling them; they might find the maroon and lilac pendants, but she was sure they would not be able to retrieve the navy pendant. It was guarded by an army of draugar. It was always around the neck of their king Moros, who was ruthless, strong, and dangerous.

CHAPTER 21

Sacrifice

Rebecca and her pack arrived at the castle. They wanted Henry to leave this place with them, but they knew he would not go as long as Catherine was alive. He wanted to be there for her and help her as much as he could before she died.

Rebecca went to see her brother. It was the first time they would properly talk since she had run away. They hadn't even spoken fully before or after the battle.

When she found him, he was in the library, sitting in his favourite chair and reading a history book she recognised. She used to be obsessed with that book; she would read it over and over when she was little. This book was about the beginning of the Gulrose Kingdom, detailing how their great-great grandfather Alexander built the kingdom and became its king.

"Hello, brother," she said.

He turned, looking shocked. He stood up, put his hands over his mouth, as he came closer to her, shaking his head.

"I can't believe you're here. I missed you so much, Becky," he said.

He hugged her, and she hugged him back, but her touch felt different. She didn't love him; she never loved him the way she loved Peter. They might have looked the same, but they were very different. After a few seconds, she separated from him.

"Yes, well, if it's alright with you, my pack and I might stay here for a bit until Catherine... well, you know. Then Henry can come with us."

"Yes, yes, he told me his plans to leave me here and run away with you," said William.

Rebecca started to walk around the library, touching all the books. She used to love this place. Whenever her father shouted at her for anything—which was often—she would hide out here and read.

"Yes, well, he should be in my pack. He needs to learn the proper way of being a manticore," she said.

William didn't agree. He believed the best place for Henry would be with him, thinking that Henry needed a male role model in his life. Rebecca, however, thought otherwise. She assured him that Henry would have plenty of male role models in her pack.

"You know, I would love to get to know your pack more. How about we have a little run through the woods tonight? Just me, you, and the boys."

Rebecca didn't want to do that. She didn't really want to spend any time with her brother unless she absolutely had to, but she knew that if they were to stay here for a little while, it would probably make everything much easier, so she agreed.

"Very well. I will let the boys and Henry know," she said.

"No, no Henry—just us."

Rebecca thought it was strange, but she didn't question it. She left to make sure the boys had rooms to stay in and promised William, she would meet him later that night in the woods.

She met her pack, and they all went room by room, settling in as she told them about tonight's plans. None of them were particularly excited about this, but like Rebecca, they thought it might not be the worst idea. They spent all day exploring the castle and training with Henry.

As the time approached for their meeting with William, they started packing up. Henry asked them where they were going, and they told him.

He wanted to join them, but Rebecca explained that William had asked to be alone with the pack to really get to know them. Henry didn't think it was strange; he just assumed William was still upset about him leaving soon.

They said their goodbyes, and the pack was on their way. It would take them about thirty minutes to reach the spot where they were supposed to meet William.

When they arrived, he was already there in his manticore form. They all quickly changed and started to speed through the forest, talking to each other as they ran.

After a while, they found themselves in the middle of the forest when they all began to slow down. A strange sensation washed over them—pain radiated through their bones out of nowhere. They were whimpering and limping, almost falling over each other, except for William, who had now shifted back into his human form. He stood behind them, watching without a hint of concern on his face.

The pack started to shift back into their human forms, but they didn't want to. It was as if they were being compelled to do so against their will. Once they were all human again, William threw each of them a coat. They put them on, and Rebecca kept asking what was going on. However, when she tried to approach William, she found she couldn't pass a certain point. They were trapped in a circle, initially obscured from view, but then fire illuminated the area around them, making it visible.

They heard someone approaching. It was a woman in her forties, drawing closer as she chanted a spell. "Do uppoffring makt overforing, do uppoffring makt overforing."

"William, what is happening?" Rebecca asked.

He looked at her with an empty expression and said, "We lost Beccy." He walked around the circle and shouted, "We lost against the filthy, evil barbarians."

He paused for a moment to calm himself. "Our father didn't lose, nor did his father, but I did. I was the first King who did not succeed. What does that say about me, huh? What will it say to all our enemies? It will say, 'Come here and take this kingdom, whose King cannot protect it.'"

The witch moved closer to William and stood beside him. "Have you got it?" she asked.

He handed her a sack of coins, which she tucked into her pocket.

"Oh, William," Rebecca whimpered.

"I must do this, Becky. I can't lose again. Never again. I am sorry."

"What do you have to do?" she asked but received no answer.

The witch began to chant once more, and the entire pack felt a pain like never before. It felt as though their bones were breaking repeatedly, as if the blood in their veins was on fire. They began to bleed from their mouths and eyes, collapsing to their knees.

"Please don't do this. Please, I am begging you," Rebecca whimpered.

"I have to. I don't have a choice." William closed his eyes, opened his arms, and looked up into the sky.

The witch kept chanting louder and louder until there was silence, and Rebecca and her pack lay dead on the ground. William's eyes turned amber. He was breathing heavily, falling to his knees, clutching his stomach. He screamed and then perked up. Opening his arms, he took a deep breath. He stood up and looked all around his body. He examined his arms and smiled, feeling the strength coursing through him.

He had sacrificed them. Losing to witches had driven him mad. He felt like a failure. He knew people whispered about him, calling him an incompetent King. He couldn't take it anymore.

Just a day prior, he had been in the library and found a book about an old legend. It told of a pack of werewolves being slaughtered by villagers because they were not strong enough to protect themselves. Many werewolves died before the alpha of the pack, named Noah, asked his friend, a witch, to perform a ritual. The five strongest werewolves of his pack agreed to be sacrificed to save their wives, their children, and the villagers. When they died during the ritual, all of their strength and speed transferred to Noah, who became a superior werewolf. No one could kill him, and he became the ultimate protector of the rest of his pack.

When William read this story, he knew this was the only way to become truly invincible. Of course, none of the witches would help him, so he needed leverage.

There was a witch living nearby with her two daughters. She hadn't got involved in the battle and had never interacted with either witches or humans. William ordered one of his best soldiers to kidnap one of her daughters, threatening the witch that if she didn't help him with the ritual, he would kill her child. Reluctantly, she complied with his demands.

"It is done. Now give me back my daughter," she said.

"Your daughter will be delivered back to your home, unharmed," William replied.

She accepted this and left. William stood there for a while, watching Rebecca and her pack lying dead on the ground. He observed the blood pouring from their open eyes.

He moved closer to them and said, "I am so sorry, Becky. I didn't want to do this, but I need the strength for everyone to fear me."

A single tear fell down his cheek, which he quickly wiped away.

"Come," he called, and an older soldier appeared from behind a tree.

"You know what to do, and don't forget: you are sworn to secrecy. Should you ever betray that promise—"

"I won't, my lord," the soldier interjected.

"Good. It would be the last thing you do."

When he looked down, he saw the maroon pendant around Rebecca's neck. He snatched it and put it around his own. He turned to walk away, but before he was completely gone, he whispered, "I love you, sister."

After he left, the soldier began to dig. He excavated five graves and placed all the bodies inside them. Once he finished, he left.

When William returned to the castle, he ran into Henry.

"Oh, hi. Where are Rebecca and the pack?" he asked.

"Henry, we need to talk," said William, leading him into the library.

Henry followed closely behind, a frown on his face. Once they arrived, William shut the door and asked Henry to sit down. He then explained that during their bonding time in the woods, at one point, it had just been him and Rebecca. She confessed that they didn't want to stay there. She told him that Henry wanted to come along with her, but she had refused. She and her pack had decided to use this opportunity to return to their home without having to explain anything to Henry or worry him further. So, she had lied, saying that William didn't want him to come.

"What? No! They wanted me to come with them, to be a part of their pack," said Henry.

"I'm sorry. I tried to convince her to stay here for you. I encouraged her to take you. Even though I wish you would stay here, I know you would learn so much more by being with them."

Henry couldn't believe that they would just leave him like this. Upset, he left the room.

William stayed behind and poured himself a glass of scotch. He could feel the power of the pack coursing through his veins. He knew that no one could challenge him now; no one would ever beat him again.

Henry went into his room and began to look through his father's diaries. He read a few pages from different years, feeling deeply betrayed by Rebecca. With all the different things happening, he had forgotten his main goal: to find his father's killer. He opened a diary from 1983, the year his father was murdered.

February 12, 1983

It will be Valentine's Day in a couple of days. I wanted to give something special to Mary, so I went to explore the market today. When I was walking through, I had that feeling again. I feel like I am going mad. This time, I saw the person following me a little bit better. I think it was a woman. It was like she wanted me to see her a little bit. She was small and had a strange walk. She walked with a little limp. Whenever I turned to look at her, she pretended she didn't see me. I did see one thing though. She had a strange mark on her hand. Possibly a birthmark? It was a decent size, black, and in the shape of a cloud. I thought it was very strange. Well, maybe I am going mad. We shall see. "

Henry couldn't believe it. A real clue to who his father's killer could be. Why did the shape of the birthmark sound so familiar to him? He couldn't remember, but he knew he had seen it before.

He began to pace around his room, thinking hard about this birthmark. He was certain he had encountered it before, but on whom?

Who? Who? Who? The question repeated in his mind over and over. He muttered to himself, "My uncle? Aiden? No, no, he said it looked like a woman. Agnes? Could be, but... oh, I don't know. Come on, Henry, think harder. Who? Who?" And then it finally clicked.

"No, it can't be."

Memories flooded back. Henry recalled one night when he and Eleanor were in the woods at their usual spot. They were lying down, enjoying each other's company, when Eleanor placed her hand on Henry's cheek. He took her hand and kissed it. That was when he noticed it—a mark that resembled a cloud. He recalled her telling him that she hadn't been born with it. When she was little, her family realised she was different from other witches; she could not perform spells and didn't display any type of magic.

They soon realised that she was what the witches would call a fon. Fons were very rare; it was possible for them to learn magic, but they would never become strong witches. That explained why Eleanor could perform simple spells, but it would take a considerable toll on her. They couldn't protect themselves or others, and so they were marked. A black cloud was magically burnt onto their wrists.

Quickly, he realised it couldn't be her; she was his age and would have been only one or two years old when this happened. Perhaps it was someone from her family who had the same mark?

CHAPTER 22
Unravelling Of The Secrets

Amara and Oliver were standing outside the Black Mansion. Oliver waved his hand, and the door swung open. As they walked in, Aiden came running down the hall to see what was happening.

"Amara! You're back?" he asked, a hint of hope in his voice.

"No, we have business to deal with here," she replied.

"What business? Please, talk to me. Tell me what's going on!"

But Amara and Oliver brushed past him, ignoring his questions. They made their way into the basement, with Aiden following closely behind. Oliver turned to make him stop, but before he could do anything, Amara stepped in and told him she would handle it.

Oliver continued walking, while Amara whispered a spell.

"Ror sig inte."

The spell caused Aiden to become glued to the ground. She knew Oliver would have done something much worse.

"I'm sorry," she said, turning away to follow Oliver. When they arrived at the spot where the spell was supposed to be hidden, Oliver made a hole in the wall. He reached inside, and after a few seconds of searching around, he found a small chest. When they opened it, there was a piece of paper wrapped in a red string.

As they unrolled it and examined the spell, they saw the words "De .....lat ......ett."

Both felt a sense of satisfaction. The spell wasn't complete, but they knew it would reveal itself fully once they found all the pendants.

"Well, that was the easiest part. We still have three pendants to find," said Amara.

"And we will. Together."

They left the basement, walked through the hallway, and out the main door. As it closed shut, Aiden was no longer stuck in place. He dashed down the basement stairs, trying to figure out what they had been doing there. He discovered the hole in the wall. While he didn't know what used to be in there or what they had just found, he was certain it couldn't be anything good. He didn't have anyone he could trust with this information, but he knew there was one person who would do anything to help him bring Amara back—Henry.

He got dressed and set off for the castle.

When he arrived, the guards wouldn't let him in. They knew exactly who he was and that he—wasn't welcome here. Luckily, Henry was just returning inside after grooming Pearl.

He approached Aiden, who was still standing outside the gate.

"What are you doing here?" he asked.

"I need to talk to you. It's important."

"I don't care. You're not welcome here."

"Yeah, I've already heard that. Look, it's about Amara. I need your help."

Against his better judgement, Henry reluctantly agreed, but he didn't invite Aiden into the castle. He knew William would not stand for it, and he didn't want to provoke another argument that day. He told Aiden to wait while he changed his clothes.

When he came back out, the guards opened the gate for him and closed it behind him. They walked into the forest to talk. Aiden explained everything that had just happened. He mentioned that he hadn't seen what they had taken, but he was certain it had to do with the pendants. Henry recalled the witch hunter speaking about them.

"But they're all lost, except for the emerald, aren't they?" asked Henry.

"My mother knew where they were. It's a sort of legacy in our family—to always know their whereabouts."

Aiden thought Amara and Oliver were going to search for the remainder of the pendants to unite them.

"Do you know where the rest are?" asked Henry.

"I don't, but there's someone who does. Someone my mother told me about, and we need to go find him."

"We? No, no, no. There is no 'we'. I hate you," said Henry.

"Yeah, I don't particularly like you myself, but I can't just give up on her. It's my fault she's like this now. I want to bring her home. Wherever that is— with me," he paused and swallowed hard. "Or you. I need her to be safe."

Henry rolled his eyes and thought about this for a second. Amara felt like a stranger to him now; the feelings he had for her before were long gone— or so he thought. Too much had happened, but she was still family, and she was in a situation that would only lead to her harm. Reluctantly, he agreed.

He told Aiden to go home, pack his bag, and they would meet back at the castle side of the forest in an hour. Henry would pack some things too, and he would take two horses, so they could venture on this journey together. Before Henry left, he asked, "Where are we going, by the way?"

"We're going to visit my mum's old teacher. He lives in Glombort."

When Henry entered the castle, he ran straight into his room. As he tried to pack all the things he might need, Lilian knocked on his door. She wanted to talk to him, as the hunters were supposed to leave the kingdom the next day, and she wanted to say goodbye. She saw Henry packing a bag frantically, and when she asked where he was going, he shared only part of the story.

"Very well. I'm going with you," she said after a moment of silence.

"No, you're not. It might be dangerous," he replied.

"Exactly! That's why you need me and my skills," she smiled.

Henry didn't really have time to argue, and to be honest, he had taken a liking to Lilian. It wouldn't be the worst thing to have her by his side.

She ran to her room, packed her bag, and met Henry in the stables.

"Did you say your goodbyes?" he asked.

"No. Did you?"

"Only to Catherine. I don't think she will be here when I come back, so I had to tell her where and why I'm leaving."

Henry took Pearl and an extra horse for Aiden. Lilian mounted her horse, Hero, and they ventured into the woods to meet Aiden.

"What is she doing here?" Aiden asked, referring to Lilian.

"I am coming with you," she replied.

"No, you're not. I don't want you here."

"Well, it doesn't really matter what you do or don't want. She's coming or I'm not," said Henry defiantly.

Aiden shot her a dirty look, jumped onto the horse Henry had brought for him, and they began their journey.

After a while, Henry turned to Aiden. "You're not going to look for your mum?"

"I want to, but I have no idea where they're hiding her. Their place is still cloaked."

An uncomfortable silence settled between them. Lilian sensed the tension and tried to lighten the mood, but her question only made things more awkward.

"So, how did you two meet then?"

"He took a girl I cared about and turned her evil," Henry replied bluntly.

"Yeah, that's what I did. Was it before or after you abandoned her numerous times and never let her be herself?" Aiden shot back.

Lilian fell silent, unsure how to respond. The rest of the journey to Glombort passed in relative quiet.

Meanwhile, Amara sat in a chair with her eyes closed and legs crossed, using Agnes's old trick with ravens to visualise the locations of the hidden pendants and assess their defences. Her concentration was abruptly interrupted by Oliver.

"We don't need my mother any longer. She's become a burden," he said, his tone dripping with a menacing implication.

Amara understood exactly what he meant: he was considering killing her. The old Amara would have fought against such an idea, but the new version of herself was indifferent. She was singularly focused on finding all the pendants and uniting them.

"Fine," she said, dismissing him with a wave of her hand. "Get out. I need to concentrate."

Oliver left the room and made his way down to the basement.

"Son, please. I've told you everything I know. Just let me go," she pleaded, her voice shaky with fear.

"So you can return to my brother and act like a happy family? I think not," he shot back, his expression cold.

"I never wanted to hurt you. I was young and foolish, please understand," Agnes begged, desperation creeping into her voice.

"I've heard that story before," Oliver replied, his indifference palpable. "But don't you get it? I don't care. You've given me all I need, and now you're of no use to me."

"Oliver, please. Don't do this," she said, but it was too late. He had made up his mind. He stepped closer to her, raising his hand.

Agnes began to choke, panic flashing in her eyes as she looked to her son, begging him silently to stop. After a torturous moment, her head dropped, lifeless. Oliver untied her, and her body slumped to the ground.

Without a trace of emotion on his face, he turned away, allowing his wolves to enter the room and feast on the remains of his mother.

When Aiden, Henry, and Lilian finally arrived in Glombort after hours of travel, they left their horses outside a tavern and went inside. They settled at a table near the window and ordered drinks and food.

As they enjoyed their beverages, the barmaid approached their table.

Aiden seized the opportunity and asked, "Do you know anyone by the name Fred Mowling?"

The barmaid's smile faded. She glanced around to ensure no one was eavesdropping. "I don't, sorry," she replied.

Aiden reached into his pocket and offered her a few coins as a bribe. "Will this help?"

Her expression shifted as she eyed the money. With a quick nod, she accepted the coins and tucked them away. "He lives nearby, in a small cabin in the woods to the east side of Glombort," she whispered before leaving their table.

The trio finished their meal, settled the bill, and stepped outside, eager to find Fred. As they emerged, they were met with an unsettling sight: four men were gathered around their horses, inspecting them with keen interest.

"Can we help you?" Henry asked, eyeing the men warily.

"Yeah, we like these horses. Think we're gonna take 'em," one of the men replied, flashing a grin that revealed a mouthful of rotten teeth.

"These are our horses, so I think not," Aiden said, stepping closer to confront them.

The men laughed and advanced toward the trio, clearly prepared for a fight. Aiden knew he shouldn't resort to magic in this place; he'd heard that locals were not fond of witches. Fortunately, he was a skilled fighter and felt confident in his abilities.

However, before either Henry or Aiden could make a move, Lilian stepped forward, taking charge of the situation. She unsheathed her favourite weapon: a long black chain with blades at the end. With a swift and practiced motion, she began to swing it around her, expertly slashing at the men's arms and legs.

Before Henry or Aiden could intervene, the men turned and fled, limping away while clutching their wounds, blood pouring from their injuries.

They both looked at her with amazed faces. Henry knew she was a great fighter, but he had never seen her do anything like this before.

Lilian noticed their expressions and said, "Well, you don't become the first in command of witch hunters unless you can hold your own."

They grabbed their horses and left quickly. When they arrived in front of the cabin where Fred was supposed to live, it was quiet—too quiet—but there was smoke coming out of the chimney, so they assumed he was home.

When they knocked on his door, he didn't open it. Instead, he simply asked who was outside and what they wanted. Aiden introduced himself and told him that Agnes was his mother. After a moment of silence, they heard around fifteen locks clicking. Fred opened the door and let them in. He made everyone some tea and asked them why they were there.

Aiden told him everything that had happened as quickly as possible.

Fred looked at him and said that it wasn't a good idea to go looking for the pendants. They should have been destroyed a long time ago. No one should have that much power.

"Please, if we find them all, we will destroy them. They have already caused too much trouble being apart; we don't want them united," said Henry.

Aiden looked at him strangely. They had never even discussed this. He didn't want to destroy the pendants.

They were his family's legacy, and he believed they should be united and stay within the family. For now, however, he decided to pretend to agree with Henry so that Fred would tell them where they were.

He took a minute to think about it and then shared the locations of each of the pendants. The emerald and amber were somewhere in the Gulrose Kingdom, and of course, Henry and Aiden already knew with whom. The maroon pendant was in Glombort with an Alpha of manticores called Rebecca. The lilac pendant was with an old witch hunter in Dodblomma, and the navy pendant was guarded in Skadlig.

He warned them about the last one. "It's guarded by the vilest enemy—someone who will crush your bones and gut you like a fish. It is guarded by draugar. Their King, Moros, always wore it around his neck, and it is impossible to get close enough to snatch it. He would kill you before you could lift your arm."

"But draugar are not real. They only live in the scary stories we were told as kids," said Lilian.

"Oh, they are real, my dear. Very real," replied Fred.

"Have you ever seen one?" asked Henry.

The truth was that Fred's wife, and child had been killed by a draugr. They usually didn't leave Skadlig; they considered it their home and had everything they needed there. But one of them had been cast out and had come here. Fred's wife and daughter were playing in the woods while he was in town, when the draugr crossed their paths. He killed them so savagely that they were almost unrecognisable.

Fred shed a few tears while telling this story. "Please, if you do find them all, you must destroy them. Too many people die every year trying to find them to gain power," said Fred.

Henry asked him how they could be destroyed and if there was a specific spell they had to use. But that, of course, wouldn't be easy. They had to unite the pendants first, and then one pendant needed to be brought to the place where they were all made—an old site at the edge of the Gulrose Kingdom. No one knew where the exact spot was. It was supposed to be where the house of Aiden's ancestors once stood. There was a legend about a map leading to that exact spot, which his great-grandfather had created in case they ever needed to destroy the pendants one day, but he didn't know where the map was. No one had ever seen it.

They thanked him and left the cabin, embarking on their journey back to Gulrose. Henry mentioned that he never knew Rebecca had one of the pendants; he had never seen it on her.

"Is she still in the castle?" asked Lilian.

"No, she is supposed to be back here. William told me that she and her pack left," replied Henry.

They decided it would make the most sense to find Rebecca here, explain the situation, and ask her for the pendant. He knew where their house was, as Rebecca had told him in one of her stories about their life there, so they changed direction and went to visit them.

When they arrived at their very large cabin, someone walked up to them from behind the house. It was a girl Henry had never seen before. She looked a bit younger than him, and it seemed like she was there alone.

She came up to them and asked, "Are you lost?"

Henry jumped off his horse, introduced himself, and asked to speak to Rebecca. The girl had a look of confusion on her face. She told Henry that the last time she saw Rebecca and the boys was when they were leaving to go to Gulrose to meet Henry. They hadn't come back yet.

"They did, they left yesterday. They should be here by now," he said.

"I am sorry, but they are not. Maybe they stopped somewhere else. They've done this before," she said.

Henry didn't like this. Nothing made sense anymore. At first, Rebecca and the boys wanted him to come with them, then they went out with William and suddenly left without Henry.

They continued their journey when Aiden decided to break the silence.

"Why aren't they here?"

Henry didn't turn to face Aiden. He shrugged his shoulders. "I don't know. They should be, but as she said, maybe they stopped somewhere else. They only left yesterday."

"Don't you think it's weird? All of this? Something isn't right," said Lilian.

Henry didn't say anything else. He knew it was strange, and he didn't really believe in what he was saying, but he didn't want another reason for Aiden to doubt William. Surely his uncle wouldn't make all of this up. What would be the purpose of that?

Why would he have to lie about them leaving if they didn't? And if they didn't leave, where were they?

"Henry, no one saw them leave. No one in the whole kingdom saw them after they left to spend the evening with William," said Lilian.

Henry's eyes flickered, and a memory came rushing back. He remembered what Rebecca had told him before she and her pack went to see William that night: "No matter what my brother says or how nice he acts, never trust him. Always doubt him. He always has a reason for everything he does, and he will kill anyone if it means he gets what he wants."

"He will kill anyone if it means he gets what he wants." This sentence played in Henry's mind over and over again. Could his uncle hurt them?

But for what reason? Maybe it was because they wanted to take Henry and Amara away, and he felt like he had no other choice.

CHAPTER 23

The Truth Always Comes Out

When they returned to the castle, Henry ran straight inside, with Lilian and Aiden following closely behind. He was looking for William, angry and ready to confront him.

He wasn't at the start, but during the journey, he had wound himself up so much that he was now furious and convinced his uncle was lying to him. When he finally found him, he told him what he had learned and asked him to tell the truth.

"I told you the truth, Henry. They left," said William.

"STOP LYING TO ME!" shouted Henry.

His heart was beating out of his chest. For the first time, he saw his uncle with open eyes and doubts in his head. He looked at the ground and then back up, his lips trembling slightly and his eyes blinking fast.

"They've never left, have they?" he whimpered.

William didn't say a word.

"Swear to me on my father that you are telling me the truth."

William took a deep breath and started to pace around the room, his hands shaking.

"I had to do it, Henry. We keep getting defeated by these filthy hexes. Yes, we won the second battle, but would we win the third, the fourth, and the fifth against them?" William pointed at Aiden.

Henry took a few steps back, shaking his head. "What have you done?"

"I had to."

Then he told Henry about the old story he had read about Noah and how his pack sacrificed themselves for the greater good, and that this was the only way.

He looked unhinged.

Henry couldn't believe it. His uncle had killed his own sister and four innocent men to gain power.

He stumbled and sat down on a sofa, massaging his forehead and rocking back and forth.

"I had no other choice, Henry, but you'll see this is a good thing. Now you and I will be unbeatable, son."

Henry looked up at him in disbelief. He stood up and walked closer to him. When he was standing right in front of him, he looked him in the eyes, chuckled, and punched him in the face. Before William could react, Aiden and Lilian stepped in between them. They knew what they both could change into, and it wouldn't be pretty for anyone—especially if what William was saying was true; he was much stronger than all three of them combined.

"I hope one day you will understand I did this for us and for the kingdom," said William before he left the room.

Henry was in pieces. He had wanted to spend some time with the pack after they found all the pendants, but he would never be able to do that now. He would never learn more about his father from her; he would never learn to be a manticore the way he could from her.

He ran to Catherine's room, screaming her name, but she wasn't there. When a maid walked in, she told him that Catherine had passed a few hours after he left. Henry sobbed as he sat on her bed, his hands slowly touching the bed sheets. So much loss, so much pain. Henry felt all alone. As he sat there in Catherine's room, Aiden and Lilian stood in front of him without saying a word.

"Well, that's it. Now there is no one to help me. No one to understand me. No one to talk to," said Henry.

Aiden sighed and replied, "Why don't we all go back to the mansion and come up with a plan on how to start looking for the rest of the pendants? We have to find them no matter what."

Henry looked at him and nodded. They went to the mansion and decided they would stay the night there before travelling anywhere.

While they were sitting in the great hall, Henry looked at Aiden.

"Aiden?"

"What?"

"You know the spell Amara used on you to bring you back to life?"

"I will not use that to bring Rebecca and her pack back, Henry. I can't."

"Why not? She did, and you're fine."

Aiden stood up and walked to the window. He looked out and said to Henry that this spell was the evilest one there was.

If you were lucky enough to survive performing this spell, your soul would be touched by evil. The devil himself would make you his puppet, and you could never come back from that.

"I never recovered. I was dead. Dead, Henry. You can't just come back to life and be okay. Ever since she brought me back, I have had this recurring nightmare. I am not myself. I am someone else now. I feel empty. "

Henry didn't say a word, and neither did Lilian. After a while, Henry spoke again.

"Well, where is everyone? It's so quiet here."

Aiden sighed. "After we lost, my mum disappeared, and Amara lost it; all the witches ran. It's just me now, all alone."

There was a brief moment between them. They didn't say a word, but they exchanged looks, as if they understood they were both on their own.

This made Aiden feel strange. He wished them goodnight and went to his room. Lilian and Henry sat there for a little while longer, talking.

"I don't trust him. He's evil," Henry said, keeping his gaze on the door Aiden had walked out of moments ago.

Lilian looked at him and leaned forward. "I don't think it's that simple. I think he has done some things he wishes he hadn't, but we've all done that. I think he feels lost, and so do you. I think we should all learn to trust each other if we are going to go on this journey together."

Henry smiled. He knew she was right. He had always despised Aiden, mostly because of Amara.

He felt like Aiden had stolen her from him and turned her into this heartless, selfish person who did evil things, but maybe he was just jealous.

"Do you believe he will help us destroy them?" asked Henry.

"I don't trust him just yet, but I want to. I want to believe everyone can change and be good. I think if I let myself, I could choose the path of evil," said Lilian.

"Why did you come with us? Why do you want to find the pendants and destroy them?"

Lilian took a deep breath and said she was here because Elias had been obsessed with the pendants for as long as she could remember. It was all he talked about, and she knew it was driving him mad. She wanted them gone. They were dangerous, and it didn't matter who they ended up with.

Suddenly, there was a loud bang. They stood up to see what was happening. They grabbed their weapons, and when they walked into the hallway, they saw them. It was Oliver and Amara.

"Well, well, weren't you all a bunch of busybodies," said Oliver.

"What are you doing here?" asked Lilian, lifting her sword.

"We are here to make sure you don't find the pendants. They belong to us. Neither of you are worthy enough to possess them," said Amara.

Lilian stepped closer to them, making it very clear that she was ready to fight.

"And you are worthy? Please don't make me laugh. A spoiled little princess who went rogue when she didn't get what she wanted. Playing with everyone around her, batting her pretty eyelashes, but when it comes to a real fight, useless."

Amara walked slowly towards Lilian, maintaining intense eye contact. "And you are? Oh yes, of course. Lilian. The great witch hunter, who never had a mother or father to love her, so she clings to the only person who could stand her but would never treat her as his daughter. You think you have a chance with someone like Henry? Is that why you're here?"

Lilian looked at Henry and then at the ground. Henry stepped forward.

"Just leave, Amara. No one wants you here, especially if you're with him."

This seemed to hurt Amara's feelings. She looked at Lilian and said, "Very well. You are first then."

Before Lilian could use her sword, Amara lifted her into the air. Lilian kicked her feet, and Henry looked up in horror.

"Amara, stop it. This isn't you!" he shouted.

Oliver had a proud smile on his face.

Henry wanted to run towards Amara and make her stop, but Oliver ensured he couldn't move. He felt completely hopeless. He couldn't help; he could only watch. The only thing on his mind was that they were both most likely about to die.

Then a knife flew by Henry's head, aimed at Oliver. Before the knife could hit him, Amara jumped in front of him. She thought she could divert the knife at the last minute, but she was too late. The knife stabbed her in the stomach, and she fell to the ground, bleeding out. Lilian suddenly dropped to the ground, gasping for breath.

When Henry turned, he saw Aiden. He was the one who had thrown the knife. Amara was wheezing, trying to breathe, clearly dying.

"Why did you do that? I could have gotten rid of it," said Oliver while he held her.

"Re... reflex, I guess," she gasped between words.

"This isn't over," said Oliver before grabbing Amara and teleporting them back to their cabin.

Henry rushed to Lilian, but she assured him she was fine once she caught her breath. Then Henry's expression changed to anger. He looked at Aiden. "What have you done?"

"I... I don't know how it happened. I aimed for Oliver. I didn't know she would jump in to protect him. They were about to kill you both." Aiden said, with a shocked expression.

They all just stood there, not knowing if Amara had survived. Henry helped Lilian up and walked her over to a sofa to sit down. "Are you okay?"

Lilian shook her head. "Yes, I am fine." She turned to Aiden. "Thank you, by the way."

There was an awkward look between Henry and Lilian. They were both very aware of the assumption Amara had made about them. Henry turned away from her and said, "We need to find out if she's okay."

"Okay, okay, I can see if she is fine, if she is safe," said Aiden.

"What? How?" Henry looked at him.

Aiden started to frantically rummage through the large desk that stood under the window Oliver had broken a few days prior, which of course was fixed by now.

"What are you looking for? Aiden. AIDEN. Let us help you," Lilian said.

"A map. I need a map."

Henry and Lilian started to look for a map, when Henry found it. "Here" He put the map on the floor.

"Give me your hand," said Aiden.

Henry looked at him and knew in an instant why Aiden wanted his hand.

"Can you cut a finger this time? Last time you cut my palm, it took ages to heal."

Aiden shot him a confused look.

"What? I need my hand intact. It's not easy to fight with a cut-up hand."

Henry put his hand above the map, and Aiden cut his finger with a small pocketknife he always had on him.

He took the finger and turned it around so drops of blood would fall on top of the map. Aiden waved his hands and said, "Lysup."

All the candles around them lit up. He took a deep breath and started the locator spell. "Ljus hitta Amara, Ljus hitta Amara."

Lilian and Henry looked at each other before Henry's eyes began to move from left to right, scanning the floor.

"Why is nothing happening?" asked Lilian.

"No, no, it can't be," said Aiden, and he tried the spell again. "Ljus hitta Amara, Ljus hitta Amara, Ljus hitta Amara."

The flames on all the candles grew stronger and bigger, then all the light was gone. Aiden ran a hand through his hair.

"What happened? Why didn't it work?" Henry asked, as if he already knew the answer.

Aiden was quiet; a tear fell down his cheek. He looked at Henry and said, "The spell only works on the living."

Even though the cabin would be cloaked, the spell would still work, showing them a large area where Amara could be, just like it had last time. But this time, the blood didn't move. It stayed still where it had dropped moments earlier.

Aiden's eyes filled with tears. "No, no, it can't be. Give me your hand again. We'll try again."

Henry shook his head. "Aiden, she's gone. She's gone, and there is nothing we can do."

Aiden stood up, still holding the knife in his hand. "I said give me your hand, or I will get the blood some other way."

Henry and Lilian quickly stood up, with Lilian stepping in between the boys. "Let's all calm down. Aiden put down the knife. "Give me the knife. Come on. She's gone. Give me the knife," Lilian said as she approached him and placed her hand on top of the knife, trying to take it away from him.

Aiden let the knife go and collapsed to his knees, staring blankly ahead. Henry stood above him and didn't know what to do. Should he be angry with him or should he let it go? Aiden had only tried to protect Lilian, despite not liking her. Amara was the one who had put herself in harm's way. It wasn't their fault she was now dead.

"You didn't aim for her. You aimed for him. She stepped in. There is nothing any of us could do," said Henry, while extending his hand to help Aiden stand up.

Aiden didn't take his hand; instead, he stood up and left the great hall. Henry closed his eyes, took a deep breath, and walked over to the sofa. He needed to sit and think. They couldn't stop their quest before it started, just because of what had happened. They had to keep going. They had to find all the pendants and end this.

Lilian could see he was worried, so she walked over to him. "What will we do now?"

"What we planned. We will leave tomorrow with or without him. We will find all of them and destroy them. We will end this."

She nodded and left to get some sleep before their big day. Henry went into the basement and walked around a bit. He looked at all the magical relics, touching them lightly. He closed his eyes, and tears began to pour down his cheeks. He thought of Amara. He thought of the sweet girl he had met on the train, the girl he was ready to risk everything for after knowing her for a day. He remembered how frightened she had been, how she had only ever wanted to be loved and understood. She had succumbed to the darkness, and before anyone could help her find her old self, she had died.

He wiped away his tears and thought of the hole in the wall in the basement. They still didn't know what they had taken that night, but they knew it had something to do with the pendants. He walked up the stairs and knocked on Aiden's door. A faint "come in" could be heard from inside. Henry opened the door and stepped in, shutting it behind him.

"Look, I know we will never be friends, and I know you feel horrible now, but you had no choice. They would have killed us all."

Aiden sat up on his bed and looked at Henry with an expression he had never seen before—heartbreak.

"But me and Lilian need you on this quest. You have knowledge we don't. You have magic, and we don't. We are leaving first thing in the morning, and I hope you will come with us." He turned to leave when Aiden stood up.

"You're right. We will never be friends, and I don't want to spend however long this takes with you and her, but I have to find all of them before my brother does."

Henry nodded and left. He went back to his room to wash up and get some sleep. He didn't know when the next time would be that he would be able to do that again.

CHAPTER 24

The Forest Of The Dead

Amara. Amara. Wake up. Come on, wake up."

Amara slowly opened her eyes. As she began to take in her surroundings, she saw Oliver kneeling next to her.

"Thank God. I would have had to do all of this alone. Too much work," he said.

Amara slowly sat up, stretched her neck, and asked, "What happened?"

"You were playing a hero, and it almost got you killed."

Amara looked at him and touched her belly. "Ah, ow, the knife. How am I alive?"

Oliver chuckled. "I am a very skilled wizard, you know. I took care of you and healed you. You will still have some pain for a few days, but you'll be fine."

"Thanks. They probably think I'm dead," she said.

Oliver stood up and told her that was exactly what they thought and that's how they would play it for a while. He enchanted Amara so that if anyone tried to perform a locator spell, it wouldn't work.

Amara didn't understand why it was necessary, but Oliver explained that it was all part of the mind games. He knew both Henry and Aiden were in love with her, and this would cause them to hate each other even more. Soon, they would stop looking for the pendants and begin to turn on one another again.

"We will leave in a few hours. Get some rest. Our journey starts soon."

Amara did as she was told and went into her room. Her stomach was sore and painful. While her wound was completely healed, touching the spot where she had been stabbed still hurt. She lay on her bed, thinking about them—about Henry and Aiden. Did they really think she was dead? She knew it would devastate them and leave them heartbroken. Should she send them a message to let them know she had survived? No, that wouldn't be a good idea. In her mind, Oliver was right; this would work to their advantage. Both would be too busy hating each other, giving her and Oliver the upper hand.

The next day, when everyone in the Black Mansion woke up, Lilian and Henry met in the great hall. They checked to make sure they had packed everything they might need for their journey and waited for Aiden to arrive.

Lilian kept glancing at the stairs, waiting for him to walk down. "Do you think he's coming?" she asked, looking at Henry.

"I don't know. It seemed to me like he would when I spoke to him yesterday."

"Maybe we should go and check on him?"

"No, he knows we're leaving and when. If he doesn't want to come, it'll just be you and me." Henry said firmly.

After a while, Henry grabbed his backpack and signalled to Lilian that they had to leave. She reluctantly took her backpack and followed him. They opened the door and shut it behind them. As they started preparing their horses, the main door swung open, and Aiden walked out, beginning to prepare his horse without saying a word. Henry and Lilian exchanged glances, and Lilian spoke first.

"We thought you might not be coming."

Aiden looked at them, his eyebrows raised. "You said seven, and oh yes, would you look at that? It's seven o'clock."

Henry rolled his eyes, and Lilian laughed it off.

"So, what's the plan?" Aiden asked.

Henry opened his map and laid it on the ground. They knew the maroon pendant was with William, the emerald with Amara, and the amber with Oliver. They would leave all of those for now and only go to retrieve the lilac and navy pendants. Once they had them, they could come back here to get the rest.

"Aren't you forgetting something?" Aiden asked.

Henry frowned, raising his eyebrows.

Aiden sighed. "Amara is gone. Oliver will have her pendant, so now he's got two. He will also try to find them all; he won't stay here."

In the end, it was decided they would stick to the original plan and go look for the lilac and navy pendants. They would deal with Oliver and William later, once they had them.

Their journey started smoothly. They passed through the whole of the Gulrose Forest without a problem. When they reached the edge of it, Aiden realised this was the furthest he had ever been. They stopped for a moment and looked behind them; they could see the castle far away, now seeming so small.

Lilian and Aiden continued while Henry stayed behind. He kept looking at the castle, remembering all the pain he had endured while he was there. He thought of Rebecca, the boys, Amara, Catherine, and his mother. As his heart grew heavier, he urged his horse forward to rejoin his companions.

When they left the forest, they rode across a wide, open field. Wherever they looked, there was nothing but miles of empty space. Suddenly, Henry stopped, jumped off Pearl, and scanned the area. Lilian and Aiden noticed this and walked over to him.

"What is it? What is going on?" asked Lilian.

Henry kept looking all around the field, his eyes wandering from left to right. "I don't know. I have a strange feeling. I feel like we are being watched."

"By whom?" She moved closer, now looking around as well.

Before Henry could answer, Aiden jumped off his horse. "No one. Look at this place. There is nowhere to hide for anyone. There's no one here. It's just you, being paranoid. Who would follow us and why? Come on, let's get going."

Lilian did as she was told, and Henry reluctantly followed. He couldn't shake the feeling that there was someone—or something—out there. After a few miles, they arrived in front of what seemed to be another forest, but it was very different from Gulrose Forest. This one was dark; the trees looked ill, all black as if they were rotting. They all stopped, though not on purpose. The horses refused to go further, stepping back.

"Ah, come on! You gave me a stupid horse, didn't you?" Aiden looked at Henry.

"I'll have you know Prissy is a great horse. It's not just her; Pearl also feels something."

Aiden rolled his eyes.

Lilian told them she had heard about this place. Elias had told her stories about a Melak Forest near the Gulrose that was home to Kvinkogs. The forest was dark, evil, and rotten. Kvinkogs were deadly spiders that could shapeshift into beautiful women or handsome men to seduce anyone they met before stinging their prey and eating them.

"That's a nice story, but how come I've never heard of this?" said Aiden.

"Well, I don't know, but we have. Hunters must know everything that can come their way so we can prepare for it and protect ourselves."

"Fine, let's say it's true. What do we do then? We have to pass through here, or we take the long way around, which would add a full day to our journey," said Henry.

They all thought about it for a second and agreed they couldn't take the long way around. They didn't have time to waste; they had to go through the Melak Forest and hope that what Lilian had just told them was a myth.

When they were only metres inside the forest, they all felt it: a strange sensation in their bones. They attributed it to being paranoid after hearing the story and kept going. When they arrived in the middle, they heard faint sobs. They all stopped to see what was going on, and then Henry saw it. It was a little girl. She was lying on the ground, crying. Henry was about to jump off his horse to go and help her, but Aiden stopped him. "What are you doing?"

"There's a child, probably lost. We need to help her," said Henry.

"No, we need to keep going. If what this one said is true…" Aiden pointed at Lilian. "It could be a trap."

"I will not leave a defenceless child in a place like this. What's wrong with you?" Henry jumped off his horse, and Lilian followed.

Aiden could tell she didn't want to, but she wouldn't let Henry go alone. He stayed on his horse, watching them and scanning their surroundings. A pit formed in his stomach, as if something was wrong, though he couldn't quite place it. Henry and Lilian were close to the little girl, who was still sobbing uncontrollably.

"Sure, go closer to the creepy girl in a creepy forest, why not?" Aiden called out behind them.

"Hey, hey, little girl. Are you okay?"

Henry slowly approached her. The girl did not answer, nor did she move. Henry looked at Lilian, who just shrugged her shoulders. He turned back to the girl and tried to speak again.

"My name is Henry. What's yours?"

The girl turned her head slightly, but they couldn't see her face, as her hair covered it.

"Henry, I don't like this. I think Aiden was right," said Lilian, glancing around as the trees began to sway.

"Henry, please…" She drew her sword, inching backwards.
Henry looked at her, then back at the girl, who was now standing with her back to him, her head bowed

low. Slowly, she turned, revealing her face—or rather, the absence of one. Henry's eyes widened, and his mouth dropped open. Lilian continued to back away, trying to reach her horse, her sword raised in defence. Henry, with one arm raised protectively, fumbled to draw his own weapon. The faceless girl started walking towards them, her pace quickening.

"Okay, okay—stay right there. We don't want to hurt you," Henry said, his voice unsteady.

But the girl kept advancing, moving faster and faster. Aiden, realising the danger, jumped off his horse to help, but just then, the girl let out a piercing scream. The sound was excruciating, forcing them all to drop their swords and cover their ears. The agony was unbearable, and they fell to the ground, writhing in pain. As the faceless girl came up to Henry, a small tail with a stinger emerged from beneath her dress, coming menacingly towards him. Henry knew he was helpless; each time he tried to lower his hands from his ears, the shriek grew louder, forcing him to cover them again. The girl continued to scream as the stinger crept closer, only inches away. In that moment, a chilling realisation struck him—if Lilian's story was true, he would be stung and devoured. For the first time, he regretted not listening to Aiden's warning.

Suddenly, something shot past them, slicing clean through the girl's head. The horrific scream stopped, leaving them in stunned silence as they staggered to their feet, ears still ringing. As they approached the fallen figure, they realised the "girl" was gone—replaced by the decapitated body of a large spider.

Henry looked down and spotted a brown knife lying nearby, its blade smeared with dark purple spider blood. Curiously, the knife had initials engraved on it: *M.V.* He picked it up, wiped it off and put it in his pocket.

"Who did that?" Lilian asked, scanning the shadowy surroundings as they hurried back to their horses.

"I don't know, but we need to get out of here, now," Aiden urged, casting nervous glances at the forest around them.

They all leapt onto their horses and sped away, Henry glancing back repeatedly, hoping to catch sight of their mysterious rescuer. *M. V.*—the initials etched on the knife would stay with him, a reminder of whoever had saved his life in those cursed woods. Once they finally broke free of the Melak Forest, they could breathe easily again.

After a little while, they stopped in a clearing, a safe spot where they could catch their breath and gather their thoughts.

"I told you it was true! I told you there were Kvinkogs in those woods," Lilian said, her voice shaky, struggling to calm her breathing.

"You said they transformed into beautiful women, not faceless, demonic children," Aiden said, jumping off his horse.

They were all visibly shaken. What had just happened could have been fatal.

"Well, I want to know who threw that blade," Aiden muttered, moving toward Henry. But Henry shook his head. All he knew was that it was someone with the initials *M. V.*

The Melak Forest wasn't far from Gulrose, meaning if someone had been following them, it was likely someone from their own kingdom.

"Maybe it was someone who lives in these woods?" Lilian suggested, glancing around nervously.

Aiden scoffed. "No one's living in a place like this, Lilian. Honestly…"

They shared a look, realising they wouldn't be getting any more answers here. Whoever had saved them could have already attacked if they'd intended to harm them. Finally, they mounted their horses again, deciding to let it go for now. Their priority was clear—they had to reach Dodblomma as soon as possible.

CHAPTER 25

The Ravine

Can we please slow down? I feel like my behind is seconds from falling off," said Henry, refusing to go any further.

Aiden stopped, turned around, and rolled his eyes. "Fine, but just for a little bit. We're far enough from the devil's forest anyway. We'll take a few minutes' break, and then we have to be on our way again."

They all jumped off their horses and stretched their legs. They had only been on the move for a few hours, but already they wanted to turn back. It felt as though something was making them more tired and irritable than usual.

Henry knew this journey would be hard, but he hadn't realised just how much. He remembered the time he'd ventured to Dodblomma before, with his uncle. They'd taken a different route. He was now curious why Aiden had chosen this one. He approached him while Lilian explored their surroundings.

"Hey, can I talk to you?"

Aiden didn't turn away from his horse. "Do you have to?"

Henry looked at him with a blank expression. "Well, I'm just going to. Why did you choose this road?"

"It's the shortest route," Aiden scoffed.

"Is it? Or did you choose it because you knew about the forest and the Kvinkogs?"

Aiden took a deep breath and stepped closer to Henry. "What are you getting at?"

Henry didn't answer, just continued to look Aiden up and down. Aiden moved even closer.

"Do you think I led us into that forest on purpose?" Aiden asked.

Henry didn't flinch; he wanted to prove he wasn't afraid. "Well, you stayed on your horse the whole time, while Lilian and I tried to help that little girl.

But you didn't. Maybe you were just waiting for her to kill us so you could speed away."

Aiden raised his eyebrows. "Why on earth would I do that?"

Henry then told him he suspected he might be working with Oliver now. He was, after all, his brother. Maybe they'd met before the trio left and struck a deal.

This made Aiden furious. He moved even closer to Henry and shoved him, causing him to fall. Henry looked up at him in disbelief but quickly got to his feet to face him again. They stood there, each ready to fight.

Henry closed his eyes, stretched his neck, and transformed into a manticore. Aiden raised his hands, ready to strike, but before either of them could do anything, Lilian stepped between them. She lifted her hands, blocking each of them from attacking.

"That's enough," she said, first looking at Aiden. "What is your problem? Why do you always have to prove something?"

Then she turned to Henry. "And you. Haven't we all had enough of death, battles, and betrayal to last us a lifetime? You need to stop doubting him and at least try to trust him."

Aiden took a few steps back. Henry walked off to hide behind Pearl. He changed back into his human form, got dressed, and returned. He looked at Aiden and said, "Look, I just want to know I can trust you. This journey we're on—it's going to be dangerous. I know we're not, and probably never will be, friends, but we have to trust each other."

Aiden managed a slight smile in agreement, though he was still irritated that Henry had accused him of working with Oliver. He and Oliver might have been biological brothers, but he knew they would never be close. They hadn't grown up together, and Oliver had taken Amara away from him. He could never forgive him for turning her into what she was now.

"We should keep going," said Lilian. "We can't keep taking breaks every hour. Otherwise, it'll take us days to reach Dodblomma."

They agreed and set off again. After a little while, they arrived at a deep, dried-up ravine. They stopped, and Lilian jumped off her horse to check if there was a way across. There was no bridge, nor anything they could use to cross, and as far as she could see, there was no way around it.

"We'll have to go down there and cross at the bottom," she said.

Henry peered down, frowning. "Are we sure there's no other way around?"

"Oh, come on, we'll be fine. We just need to be careful. It'd take ages to find another route, if there even is one," Aiden replied.

Fortunately, a narrow path led down the ravine. They decided the safest way to descend would be to walk their horses rather than ride them. Lilian went first, Aiden followed, and Henry took up the rear. They were halfway down when the path narrowed. They slowed their pace, and Lilian turned back, a worried look on her face.

"It's alright," said Aiden. "Just go step by step, slowly, and watch where you're putting your feet."

She took a deep breath and moved carefully. A few steps later, she felt something shift under her right foot. Before she could react, the ground beneath her crumbled. She lost her grip on Hero's reins and fell through the ground.

"Lilian!" Henry shouted, carefully edging towards where she had been moments before. When he looked down, he saw her clinging to a rock, dangling over the drop.

"Help! Pull me up!" she called, her grip slipping. Henry lay flat on his stomach, stretching his arm out to reach her, but it wasn't enough. Aiden quickly grabbed Henry's arm, giving him extra few inches. Lilian stretched her free hand toward Henry, her eyes wide with fear. "Come on, grab my hand!"

"I'm trying, I can't reach!" Henry's fingers were just inches away.

They nearly touched when, suddenly, Lilian lost hold of the rock and plunged into the ravine.

"Lilian!" Henry's heart sank as he watched her fall. For a split second, he saw the terror in her eyes as she reached up instinctively, her expression braced for impact.

"Noooo!" he shouted, but it was too late. She plummeted toward the rocky ground below. But just before she struck, her body stopped an inch from the ground. Eyes wide, Lilian blinked, confused as she realised, she was floating.

Henry turned to Aiden and saw him with his arms outstretched, chanting under his breath, his gaze fixed on Lilian. Slowly, Aiden lowered her until her feet touched the ground, and then he slumped to his knees, exhausted.

Henry let out a shaky breath, then chuckled in disbelief. He turned to Aiden. "Are you alright?"

Aiden gave a weak smile. "Yeah, why?"

Henry shook his head in relief. "You just saved her life. I didn't know you could do... whatever that was."

Aiden shrugged, looking a little embarrassed. "Neither did I, really."

"You're bleeding." Henry pointed at Aiden's nose.

Aiden touched beneath his nose, and when he looked at his fingers, he found them smeared with blood. The spell had taken a toll on him; it wasn't easy to catch a person in mid-air with his powers, especially at the speed Lilian had been falling.

"Come on, we have to get down there," Henry urged.

"I know, I just need a second," Aiden replied, sliding down to rest his back against the rocks. Henry moved to Pearl and tied her reins to Prissy.

"Come on, get up. We have to go," Henry said, offering Aiden his hand.

Aiden stood, and together they began to make their way down. When they reached the bottom, Lilian ran to Henry and hugged him tightly. He smiled and embraced her back.

"I thought you were gone when I saw you, falling," he said, his voice laced with relief.

"I know, but luckily I'm not," Lilian replied, releasing him to turn her gaze to Aiden. "Thank you for saving me."

They jumped back on their horses and continued their journey. After another few hours, they finally arrived at Dodblomma. The only person who had been there before was Henry. He remembered where they had gone to see the hunters but didn't know where to look for the old man who was supposed to be guarding the lilac pendant.

"Where is this guy supposed to live?" Henry asked.

"At the edge of the Dodblomma Forest," Aiden replied, studying their map. "Which is… hmmmm… oh, here it is." He pointed to a spot on the map.

"Have you ever heard of him?" Henry asked Lilian.

"Yes, a few times, but no one has ever seen him. We didn't even know if he was alive or even real."

After fifteen minutes or so, they arrived. They saw a small brown cottage with a black roof. The windows were bolted, and it looked like no one was home. They jumped off their horses, tied them to a tree, and walked over to the door. Lilian knocked, and they all took a few steps back. The door opened slightly, and they heard a man's voice.

"Who are you? What are you doing here? What do you want?"

"Are you Ezekiel?" asked Lilian.

"Who wants to know?" he replied.

Henry stepped forward and introduced each of them. He explained that they were there because of the lilac pendant and asked if they could come in. Lilian added that she was also a hunter and that her mentor was named Elias.

The man hesitated for a moment but then reluctantly opened the door. They all walked in, Ezekiel shut the door behind them, locking it straight away. He wondered why they were there for the pendant and why they thought he would give it to them willingly.

"We want to find them all and destroy them," said Henry.

"Do you think you're the first ones to claim that?" Ezekiel said, crossing his arms.

Many had come before, trying to obtain this pendant and the others. Many had promised they would destroy them all, but Ezekiel knew they never would. He could read people in a way no one else could.

Henry stepped closer to him. "We're telling you the truth. How can I prove it to you?"

"There is nothing you can say," Ezekiel replied, shaking his head.

Henry sat down; his head bowed. He looked at Ezekiel with a hopeful glimmer in his eyes. "Please, I didn't come all the way here from London thinking I would have to do this, but here I am. I didn't expect to be chasing a ghost with a cloud tattoo, one who might or might not have murdered my father."

"What did you say?" Ezekiel interrupted.

"That I didn't come from London," Henry replied, confused.

"No, not that part. The other part about the tattoo."

Henry's eyes widened. He told Ezekiel the entire story—about his father's diaries and the tattoo of the person described in them. Ezekiel's gaze darted around the room, as if searching for something he couldn't quite find. He stood up, walked over to his small library, and pulled out a book. Returning to his seat, he showed Henry a piece of paper. On it was a drawing of the tattoo Henry had described—the same tattoo he had seen on Eleanor and the one mentioned in Peter's diaries.

Ezekiel explained that there was an old tale, like a prophecy. It was said that nearly a hundred years ago, a very dangerous enchantress would find all the pendants, unite them, and destroy all of Mörkdimma. She would bring fire and death upon everyone and rule all the kingdoms with an army of draugar behind her.

Lilian, Aiden, and Henry exchanged glances. Henry's hands trembled, and a shaky voice escaped him. "Well, it's just a story, right?"

He shook his head. He told Henry it wasn't just a story; the woman who predicted it was a seer, capable of seeing the future.

"But how do you know when it's supposed to happen? She predicted this almost a hundred years ago, you said. Why hasn't it already happened?" asked Lilian.

Ezekiel sighed. "It was foretold that it would occur when the fire comet is visible, which happens every hundred years in Mörkdimma."

"The fire comet?" Henry's interest peaked.

Ezekiel launched into another tale—the story of the first fire comet. It had appeared in Mörkdimma over a thousand years ago. The original witches who lived there performed a spell that night to bring their dead leader back to life. They knew the spell might cost them their lives, as only the strongest would survive. However, they did not anticipate that the fire comet would grant them the strength to complete the spell, and by that coincidence, they discovered the comet's power. Since then, for any spell requiring a significant amount of magical energy, the fire comet has been invoked. For something as grand as uniting all the pendants, the most powerful magical tool of all would be essential.

"When is the next fire comet coming?" asked Lilian.

He took a deep breath. "In twenty-three days from today, on Friday, 12th of January. That's when the next fire comet is supposed to appear."

"Well, that's not a lot of time," Henry said, rubbing his hands together.

"No, it's not. I was preparing for the end of everything, accepting our fate, but maybe there is a chance to stop all of this. If you can find all of them and destroy them, it could save us all."

Ezekiel stood up and motioned for them to follow him. They descended into his basement, where he opened a safe. Inside, there was a small box. Ezekiel took it out and placed it on top of a table. The room fell silent as everyone watched him intently. He took out a small pocketknife and cut his finger, allowing blood to drip onto the box. He then pressed his bleeding finger against the lock and waited. They heard a click, then Ezekiel opened the box, retrieving a small pouch. He handed it to Henry, who opened it, and gasped as he revealed the lilac pendant. He examined it curiously for a moment before placing it around his neck.

"Hold on, I should be the one wearing it," said Aiden.

"Why? It's perfectly safe with me," Henry replied.

Aiden stepped closer, inches from Henry's face. "My family made these; it's my heritage."

Ezekiel intervened, positioning himself between them. "I think it's safer with Henry. The pendants affect witches in different ways."

"Come on, Aiden, we're all in this together, right?" Lilian added, attempting to call Aiden down.

Aiden took a few steps back and nodded reluctantly. Ezekiel turned to Henry and cautioned him, "Be careful, boy. These are not just pretty jewels."

"They have evil in them; they corrupt people and their hearts. Always remember your true purpose: to destroy them."

Ezekiel handed Henry a piece of parchment on which the prophecy was written.

"Read this. It will tell you everything you need to know. Only one person can defeat the enchantress—

the one who bears the mark you mentioned. Find him or her, just in case you need them."

Henry nodded and touched the pendant, feeling its weight against his chest. He hid it behind his shirt, and the three of them set off on their way. Their next stop? Skadlig.

CHAPTER 26

The Supreme One

When they left Dodblomma, there was an uncomfortable silence once again. Henry was thinking about the prophecy and the person who was supposed to help them all—the one who could defeat the enchantress.

It would take them three days to arrive at Skadlig, and they didn't even know what they were getting themselves into. They only had twenty-three days to stop all of this: to find all the pendants, unite them, and destroy them. Everyone they had spoken to warned them about what lived there, and Henry really didn't want to face them.

After a few hours, they stopped, knowing they would need all the rest they could get. They sat down in the middle of a small forest and took out some food for themselves and for the horses. No one spoke for a while until Lilian cleared her throat. "I think Amara is the enchantress."

"We don't know that." Aiden said.

"No, I think she's right. It's either her or your mother, but I am willing to bet everything on Amara. I think she survived; I don't think she's dead. Oliver would not let her die. He needs her," said Henry.

Aiden stood up and walked around them, back and forth. "Okay, then we have to make sure she doesn't do what she is supposed to do according to this prophecy, which might not even be true."

"Amara sealed her own fate when she decided to follow Oliver," Lilian suddenly stood up.

Aiden looked at her, his jaw tightening.

"That doesn't mean we aren't going to help her, and I don't need your permission for that."

They both looked at Henry, as if they were waiting for him to be the tiebreaker, but he didn't say a word. He was conflicted between the two. He didn't want to hurt Amara if she was alive, but he couldn't risk everyone's lives and freedoms for her.

"Well, I want to know who this mystery person is, who is supposed to help if it comes to that." Said Henry.

"Who knows? I don't care. We don't need anyone else. More people mean more trouble. We've already adopted this one," Aiden said, looking at Lilian.

"Charming, as always," she rolled her eyes.

"Okay, let's get some sleep. I will take the first watch," said Henry.

While Lilian and Aiden slept, Henry walked around. He wanted to clear his head, but he also knew that if he sat down, he would just fall asleep, so he read the prophecy again.

"An all-powerful enchantress shall find and unite the most powerful jewels during the next comet of fire. She shall bring flames and death upon all Mörkdimma. She shall rule and destroy. The supreme one will have the power to vanquish her and to keep the peace. They shall possess a kindness like no other and bear the mark of a cloud. May the heavens protect all."

He needed to know who the supreme one was. Who would be powerful enough to face Amara and Oliver? He read the prophecy over and over again. He knew the mark was placed on people with limited powers. How could someone like that defeat them? With what power?

Before he knew it, he couldn't stay awake any longer; it was time to wake Aiden for the next watch. When Henry finally lay down on the hard ground, he fell asleep instantly. As soon as he was asleep, he had a dream that felt very real. He saw a woman, her back turned to him, with long brown hair and a black dress. Flames surrounded her, but she never turned to face him. He saw a tall man with brown hair standing behind her as she cast fire all over the Gulrose Kingdom. The kingdom was in flames, the sky was black, and screams filled the air. Men, women, and children were on the ground, dead.

The man slowly approached her and plunged a silver dagger right through her heart from behind. As she fell to the ground, the kingdom returned to normal. The sun shone, and laughter filled the air. Henry couldn't see the man's face; all he could see was his right arm and a cloud tattoo on his wrist. He woke up, breathing heavily, sweat dripping down his neck.

Aiden stood up and walked over to him. "What is it?"

Henry looked at him, trying to catch his breath. "I had a dream about the prophecy. We need to find the supreme one."

They woke Lilian, and then Henry told them about his dream. He explained that the person who could defeat the enchantress was a man. He couldn't see his face, but he knew it was him—the one they had to find.

"Okay, well even if that's true, we can't look for the pendants and for him," said Aiden.

"We have to. We could try to search for both." Henry looked at Lilian.

"No, Aiden is right. We don't have time for that, Henry, and if we find all the pendants and destroy them, we won't need him," said Lilian.

Aiden's eyes widened in disbelief that she actually took his side. Frustrated, Henry walked away.

Aiden rolled his eyes and followed him. "Where are you going? We have to get back on the road soon."

Henry didn't say a word; he sat down and rested his arms on his knees. Aiden sat next to him and shook his head. "Do you even remember her?"

"Who?" asked Henry.

"You know who—Amara."

Henry's eyes glittered. "I can't allow myself to remember."

"We have to help her, Henry. She went down the wrong path, but she would help you if this happened to you."

Henry looked down and pulled out the lilac pendant from behind his shirt. He took it off and kept staring at it.

"All of this because of something so small. How can this one and the others be so powerful?"

"My ancestors had a lot of power, and they put it into the pendants. They made them mainly to protect themselves."

"Protect?" Henry stood up, clenching his fists. "They had so much power that if Amara gets all of them, she will destroy not only Gulrose but the whole of Mörkdimma. I would do anything to protect her, but not if it means putting others in danger."

Aiden faced Henry; his chin held high. "That's the difference between you and me. You say you would do anything to protect her unless you have to hurt another person, but I would kill thousands of people to make sure she was safe."

Henry looked at him one last time before going back to Lilian and their horses to continue their journey. What Aiden said concerned him. He knew how much Aiden loved Amara, and though he wasn't the nicest person, it was now clear that no one was safe when it came to her. Aiden might even betray Henry in this quest if it involved Amara.

They all jumped back on their horses and continued on their journey to Skadlig.

Amara was standing on top of a hill, looking at the Gulrose Kingdom. She was gazing far into the distance, her eyes glittering. She was rethinking everything she had done. It was as if, when she had almost died, her perspective had changed a little bit. It affected her. She suddenly hated herself for the way she had hurt the people she loved and cared about: Henry, Aiden, her mum, and even Agnes. Yes, she wasn't the nicest person and had only used them, but she didn't deserve to die for that. She knew there was no coming back. There was nothing she could do now for the people she cared about most, nothing to make them trust her again. She knew Aiden would never forgive her, he wouldn't even look at her when he found out his mother was dead, and Amara let it happen.

"Amara, it's time to go," Oliver called out to her.

She wiped away her tears and went over to him. He was standing next to two horses. Oliver's horse was white, named Wolf, and Amara's horse was black, named Storm. They packed everything they might need, from food to weapons, and set off for Dodblomma to retrieve the lilac pendant. Of course, they didn't know that Henry, Aiden, and Lilian were on the same journey as them and that they already had the pendant. They rode through the Gulrose Kingdom, with Oliver's wolves behind them. They had never had much of a deep, meaningful conversation before. Amara wanted to get to know him more; she needed to know she could trust him.

"Can I ask you something?" she said.

"Sure."

"Why did you kill Agnes?"

Oliver was quiet. Amara looked at him and said, "I know she made a mistake when you were little, but she was still your mother. You must have felt something for her."

Oliver looked at her and smiled. "Amara don't look for some kind of kindness or compassion in me. I did not love her, and I did not care when I killed her. She had to die, and it meant nothing to me."

Amara swallowed hard. She couldn't believe it. Was he really this evil? She quickly realised it didn't matter. She just needed to get the pendants, unite them, and rule; she only needed him for the journey. Oliver thought they would rule together, but Amara had a different idea. She couldn't imagine having to deal with Oliver and his temper. She knew she couldn't do all this alone, but once they achieved all they wanted, she would make his wolves hers, and she would be the one true ruler. She knew she would have to make sure Henry and Aiden either joined her or left Mörkdimma, but she wasn't too concerned with them right now. She thought they didn't have what it took to rule the kingdom.

When they arrived in Dodblomma to get the lilac pendant from Ezekiel, they knocked on his door, but no one opened it. With one wave of her hand, Amara blasted the door open. When they stepped inside, the house was a mess, with chairs and tables knocked over, and plates and mugs smashed on the ground. They walked up to a room that turned out to be Ezekiel's bedroom, and when they opened the door, they saw Ezekiel. He was hanging from the wall; the only thing that kept him up there was a sword through his heart.

"Well, he won't be able to help us," said Oliver.

"Stating the obvious," Amara said, coming closer to Ezekiel and inspecting his face and body. She turned to Oliver and said, "It had to be them."

"Who?"

"I thought you were smart. Henry and Aiden. They might have found out about everything. Who else would be hunting the pendants?"

They realised they didn't have as much time as they thought. They had to go to their next stop. They had to arrive in Skadlig as soon as possible. They jumped on their horses and continued their journey.

Just as Oliver and Amara found out about them, Lilian, Aiden, and Henry finally arrived at Skadlig. They stood on top of a hill overlooking it. They could see an enormous mountain. It covered most of Skadlig and they knew that was where all the draugar were.

Before they would even try to go in and get the pendant, they knew they had to assess the situation. They had to know how large an army was hiding inside and what chances they stood. It was decided they would set up a camp nearby and try to figure out their next steps. As they were about to leave, they looked at the mountain one last time, and that's when they saw it. A giant draugr emerged. His body was covered in black armour, and a black crown sat on his head. His face petrified them. They had never seen anything like him before.

Dark, evil eyes and death-like black skin. The three of them stood side by side, shocked by the sight in front of them. Fear filled their bodies; they could feel it in their bones.

It was him. Moros.

THE LOST PENDANT

Copyright © 2024 by SUZIE JAY